MOLLY : THE HIGHLAND CLAN , BOOK 6
Published by Keira Montclair
Copyright © 2016 byKeira Montclair

This is a work of fiction. Names, characters, places and incidents
are either the product of the author's imagination or are used
fictitiously, and any resemblance to actual persons, living or dead, business establishments, events or locales is entirely coincidental.

Printed in the USA.

Cover Design and Interior Format

Molly

THE HIGHLAND CLAN   SIX

KEIRA
BESTSELLING AUTHOR
MONTCLAIR

THE GRANTS AND RAMSAYS IN 1280S

GRANTS

LAIRD ALEXANDER GRANT, and wife, MADDIE
John (Jake) and wife, Aline
James (Jamie)
Kyla
Connor
Elizabeth
Maeve

BRENNA GRANT and husband, QUADE RAMSAY
Torrian (Quade's son from his first marriage) and wife, Heather-Nellie
and son
Lily (Quade's daughter from his first marriage) and husband, Kyle-twin
daughters
Bethia
Gregor
Jennet

ROBBIE GRANT and wife, CARALYN
Ashlyn (Caralyn's daughter from a previous relationship) and Magnus
Gracie (Caralyn's daughter from a previous relationship)
Rodric (Roddy)
Padraig

BRODIE GRANT and wife, CELESTINA
Loki (adopted) and wife, Arabella-sons, Kenzie and Lucas
Braden
Catriona
Alison

JENNIE GRANT and husband, AEDAN CAMERON
Riley
Tara
Brin

RAMSAYS

QUADE RAMSAY and wife, BRENNA GRANT (see above)

LOGAN RAMSAY and wife, GWYNETH
Molly (adopted)
Maggie (adopted)
Sorcha
Gavin
Brigid

MICHEIL RAMSAY and wife, DIANA
David
Daniel

AVELINA RAMSAY and DREW MENZIE
Elyse
Tad
Tomag
Maitland

CHAPTER ONE

IN MOLLY RAMSAY'S EYES, THIS was one of the worst, most dreaded things that could ever have happened to her. She closed her eyes and took a deep, cleansing breath since her mama had taught her it was the only way to get through the most difficult situations life could throw at you.

It didn't help. There was no way out.

Slud, shite, hellfire, what other curse word could she come up with?

She put one foot in front of the other, the pace of her breathing increasing with each step that brought her closer to her fate.

There must be something she could do.

Something!

As her gaze searched for a way out, a hand pushed at her back.

"You can do this." Her mother's voice urged her forward.

Her sister, Sorcha, tugged her hand and yanked her toward her living hell.

She wished to fight this with every smidgen of her being. *Nay! Please do not make me!*

She cast her mother one final glance over her shoulder.

Her sire said, "Gwynie, she's so much like you." His chuckle rankled her.

Molly spun around to give her adoptive father a blistering glare and he covered his mouth in a sore attempt to hide his amusement. Her adoptive mother, Gwyneth, whom she adored as much as she did her sire, whispered, "Stop that now, Logan, or you'll find out a few more things about your wife you have not learned yet."

"Gwynie, you are so beautiful in your gown. I love your leggings more, but you'll make all the ladies jealous when they see you." He leaned down to kiss her cheek, a small grin on his face.

Molly glanced over her shoulder to see what her mother's response would be to her father's compliment, but she instead ignored their small battle and returned her attention to the horror that was about to take place in front of her.

Nay!

Stop!

Help me, someone please help me!

Do not make me do this.

When her foot stepped inside the doorway, she closed her eyes, wishing she could disappear. Too late. They could all already see her.

King Alexander had declared this to be a night of celebration, and invited all to attend his court in the royal castle of Edinburgh. Her parents had done the unthinkable and forced her to attend, *and* they'd coerced her into doing something far worse, something she'd never, ever, *ever* willingly do.

She was dressed in a forest green gown, tight across the bodice, with gold threading and ribbons everywhere. How she missed her tunic and leggings, the ones she wore just like her mother always did.

Her sire, Logan Ramsay, whispered from beside her, "Molly, you are no longer that lass we found in Edinburgh. You are beautiful, strong, and talented. Believe it. Believe in yourself."

Her mother said, "He's right. Forget your true father. You are beautiful."

How she wished she could believe them, but she knew it to be a falsehood. Her true sire hadn't held back when he'd jabbed her with cruel, barbed insults about her looks. There was a reason she'd spent a lifetime refusing to look at her own reflection in the loch water as her sisters loved to do. And yet here she was, in a gown, allowing her parents and her beloved little sister to lead her through the royal great hall full of lads, something akin to torture for her.

Her father led them to a table near the dais at the middle of the hall. "Sit here, lassies. Your mother and I will be seated at the dais." He gave Sorcha a pointed look. "We will not be far, daughter, so you'd best keep that in mind."

Sorcha frowned before reverting back to her usual smile. "Father, there is no reason for you to worry about us."

Her father merely snorted at her. Did their sire know more than Molly thought he did? Was he aware of Sorcha's flirting and teasing ways, or that Molly loved to go along with Sorcha? The truth was that they both liked to talk to the lads, but Molly preferred to focus on certain ones, and never, ever in a gown. Why did the heavy garment make her feel so plain and out of her element?

Either way, Molly's legs were trembling enough that she feared falling clumsily to the floor, in front of everyone at the royal castle, so she fell onto the bench gratefully.

Sorcha tugged on her arm. "Molly, we must mingle."

Molly did not move, nor did she glance at her sister. Neither the King of England, the King of the Scots, nor a charging bear could move her from this spot. She would not embarrass herself any further by roaming around the hall where all the lads could see her. Not once had she been in anything but her leggings in Edinburgh before this day. Why did things have to change?

Her mother reached for her hand and squeezed it. "Why do you not talk to some of the other young people here? Mayhap you would enjoy making new friends."

She shook her head in denial. "Mama, I choose not to mingle. I am too uncomfortable to talk to others, and there is no reason to make new friends when we are here on a specific assignment. I will not be back here any other day with a gown on in the great hall. Besides, what if...?"

"What if?" Her mother waited for her reply, her gaze patient but unwavering.

"What if someone knows me, or someone recognizes..." Her voice trailed off. She was so unsure of herself. Years ago, she'd been sent away from her home in England by her true father. He'd believed he had too many mouths to fill, so he'd chosen to send one away in servitude. Molly, whose hair he'd deemed too wild, whose face he'd deemed too plain, had been his first choice, though her mother had insisted on sending her sister, Maggie, with her so she'd never be alone. They'd been sold as housemaids to an English family that punished their maids for the slightest transgression.

Gwyneth Ramsay had found her tethered to a tree just outside of Edinburgh Castle. She'd been left there as part of a punishment, the first part of which had involved the bad end of a switch. As soon as Gwyneth had learned of Molly and Maggie's horrible living conditions, she'd immediately requested to adopt them. Molly's adoptive parents were the greatest gift she had ever received in her life, and she'd vowed never to be far from one or the other. Her heart would not tolerate it.

Every night, her first prayer to the Lord was that Logan and Gwyneth Ramsay would never give her away.

"Papa, Molly and I would like to find Coll and Tormod, if you do not mind." Sorcha pointed over her mother's shoulder.

Seven guards from Clan Grant had just ridden in from Grant land in pursuit of Ranulf MacNiven, a man who had escaped his own hanging and threatened to take over the Highlands. Jamie Grant, the laird's son, Braden, Coll, Tormod, and Art had traveled from Clan Grant and met them in Edinburgh to do as their king had instructed and find MacNiven's location. Two others had been with them, Magnus and Ashlyn, but they'd gone back to the Highlands due to Ashlyn's injuries. MacNiven was still free, though, and now they waited to see where the king would send them next.

Her father narrowed his gaze on Coll and Tormod, who'd just entered the hall together. "You have my permission. 'Tis early in the night, but behave like a lady, if you please. Remember, no leggings, no belching."

"Papa," Sorcha mumbled, "must you mention my secrets? Please do not. How am I to catch a lad if he learns of my awful habit?"

Molly giggled at her sire. Sorcha did indeed have a bad habit of passing foul air around others. Her mother chastised her for it frequently. When she'd been young, it had been a game. Molly had always thought her sister would outgrow it eventually, but while she did refrain from belching around lads, she rarely contained herself around her family.

Sorcha tugged her hand, and they headed toward the Grant lads, taking the long way around. Her sister leaned over to whisper in her ear, "Since we're in Edinburgh, why not look at the other lads who are here? I love to look for the strongest and the most handsome lads, do you not?"

Molly gave the loudest sigh she could, hoping her sister would take the hint. "Nay. I am not interested in finding the most handsome lad in this crowd, not wearing this dreadful thing." She flounced her skirts, wishing she could tear them off from the waist down. "I know we've teased lads before to get information, but not here, not in this setting. I have other goals for this trip."

"Molly, sometimes you are too serious. And today, you talk as if you were a lad."

"Mayhap I would prefer to be a lad. Besides, catching the biggest villain in decades is serious. I aim to put an end to MacNiven's treachery or be with Mama when she finds him."

Sorcha smiled at a few lads who had stopped in front of them, but she skated around them, ignoring their inviting gazes. "I hate it when you say that. You are an asset to womanhood. You are almost as good an archer as our mother. We need strong Scottish women. Even though you were born English, we claim you as a Scot. You know our sire loves to brag about you to the Scottish Crown."

They were still making their way around the chamber when two lads stopped them. The taller one said, "My, but are you not a beautiful lass? Why have I not seen you before?" His eyes widened as his gaze traveled from Sorcha's head to her toes and back up again.

Sorcha gave him a half smile. "Because we are not oft in Edinburgh."

"Perfect." His friend gave him an elbow in the side. "Excuse me, er... that is sad. I wish you lived here so I could court you. I am the son of a baron. Perhaps we could meet later tonight." He leaned closer and whispered, "I'll come outside your window if only you'll tell me how to find it."

The lad's friend stared off into the distance before wandering off. His friend had staked a claim on Sorcha, and he was not interested in Molly, so he'd left to look for another. Molly was used to being ignored, especially around her younger sister. While Sorcha's rich, bronze-colored hair fell in soft waves when she set it free, Molly's dark hair was so curly it formed knots. Her plain brown eyes matched her brown hair, whereas her sister had brilliant green eyes. Even their frames set them apart—Sorcha had the curves a lad desired, and Molly was tall and lean. She hadn't thought her breasts would ever grow, but they'd finally blossomed a few years ago. Still, they were not the size of Sorcha's.

At least she was no longer man-chested, as she'd been called in the past. And at least she was not the target of such open attempts at seduction. Sorcha could handle herself, though, so Molly took the time to glance at her surroundings, at the rich tapestries on the wall, many of them a regal red. The tables were decked out in red linens and golden serve ware.

"Forgive me," Sorcha said to the flirtatious lad, "but my father, Logan Ramsay, would not like that. I would be happy to direct you to *his* window."

The lad blushed a deep shade of red and spun on his heel. Logan and

Gwyneth's reputation was well known throughout Edinburgh.

Molly smirked. "You frightened another away."

"I know. Sometimes 'tis useful to have parents who are known to all." She tugged on Molly's hand and led the way to Coll. "Good eve to you, Coll."

Coll pivoted and his face lit up. "Good eve to you, Sorcha. Greetings, Molly."

Art had just ambled up to the lads, a strange smile on his face, and he and Tormod each nodded to them in greeting. Tension oozed from the three of them, especially from Tormod toward Art. What could have happened between them inside the Royal Castle? Of the three, Molly thought Tormod was the nicest and the best-looking. Coll was handsome, too, but Art? There was something a wee bit untrustworthy about him. Whatever the disagreement between them, she would wager that Tormod and Coll had the right of it.

Molly was not interested in any of them at the moment. If she were not on assignment, she could have been interested in Tormod, but she needed to focus on her work. Besides, he would prove to be a distraction, something she could not afford. This was the perfect opportunity for her to achieve her lifetime goal.

"Does my sister not look beautiful in her gown?" Sorcha asked.

Molly grabbed her sister's arm and squeezed it in an attempt to silence her. Sorcha *knew* how much she hated drawing attention to herself. The three lads looked at Molly at the same time, each nodding in approval. Only Tormod spent more than a second taking in her appearance. Even so, she blushed at their perusal.

"Ow!" Sorcha glared at her. "I was only trying to be nice," she whispered under her breath.

Their sire suddenly popped up behind them, and Molly couldn't have been more pleased.

"Lads, you are well this eve?" Logan Ramsay loomed over most of the lads in the room, but he was about the same height as Tormod. His shoulders had not lost any of their intimidating breadth. He kept his brown hair long, just as he always had, but there was now a touch of gray at his temples. His eyes were the same brilliant green eyes as Sorcha's.

Coll replied, "Aye. Do you think Magnus and Ashlyn shall have any difficulties?"

"Mayhap with the weather. I heard there was a storm about a day north. I believe they can handle any difficulties." Her father had a famil-iar gleam in his eyes—one that told her that he was not unaware of the impression he made on the lads, who'd all taken a few steps back from Sorcha.

"My lord, will you spar with us before we begin our search on the morrow?" Coll's expression was hopeful. "The practice would do us good."

Molly's sire's grin matched the glimmer in his eyes. "Naught would please me more than to beat your sorry hides in swordplay. On the mor-row, we shall see to it."

Molly could see the excitement in the lads' eyes. Hellfire, but she wished she could practice swinging a sword. She had tried to lift her sire's sword once and it had almost knocked her over. She just did not have the arm strength for it. Her mother did not either, but she had no interest in swordplay.

Molly envied the lads and wished to be able to do everything they did.

Her true sire had seen no value in her or Maggie. Somehow, she had to make sure that Logan Ramsay saw her differently. She wished to be his daughter forever.

And while she never wished to see her true sire again, she would give anything to do something so wonderful and unexpected that her true sire would hear about it back in England.

She wanted, more than anything, to make him regret giving her and her sister away.

CHAPTER TWO

TORMOD MORISTON HAD HALF A mind to kill Art.

Not too long ago, he and his clanmates Jamie, Braden, Coll, and—alas—Art had been standing in the courtyard of Edinburgh Castle. "Are you not all going to the entertainment in the great hall this eve?" he'd asked the others.

"I am," Coll had said, much to his relief. He felt most comfortable with Coll. Jamie and Braden were both part of his laird's family, and Art...well, the less he had to think about him, the better. "Shall we take our leave?"

"Aye," Tormod had replied, anxious to get inside to see a certain lass who'd caught his eye. "I am so hungry I could eat the hide of a hairy boar."

Art, wearing his usual smirk, said, "Aye, I'll come along for some entertainment."

Coll pivoted to speak to him. "There is no entertainment. We're here as guests of the king. The only reason we go inside is to eat. I know your ways, and you're after trouble. Not tonight."

Art said, "Nay, I wish to eat. 'Tis all. I'll wait if you two prefer to go alone." He'd guffawed at his own sour humor, but then Art had insisted on coming with them, and Tormod's happy anticipation of the feast had crumbled to ashes. Jamie had told them that he and Braden would join them inside after talking with the guards to see if aught was stirring in the royal burgh.

Tormod remembered all too well what happened next.

Just as he, Art, and Coll moved toward the doors, Art whispered to him, "I'd wager you're hoping to get between Molly Ramsay's thighs on this trip, just as Coll is aiming for Sorcha's maidenhead."

Tormod spun around and grabbed Art's chest, slamming him against the stone of the castle wall. "Do not say such things about Molly or Sorcha, or you'll be feeling my fist between your teeth. Go back home if 'tis all you can think about."

Art's eyes lit up as a wicked grin crossed his face. "I hit a tender spot, aye? My guess is that you favor Molly. Mayhap I'll go for a dive first."

Tormod swung his fist back, ready to plant it in Art's face, but Coll's hand caught his fist first. "Not here. I know his mouth is foul, but not at the royal castle. Logan will skin us if you cause trouble."

"Then tell the bastard to keep his mouth closed. If Logan Ramsay ever catches what he says, he'll be a dead man." Tormod wanted nothing more than to smash the fool's face in.

Coll shrugged his shoulders. "Then allow Logan to take care of him. He's not worth the effort, he'll never change. You know he tries to goad you, and you'll react. The king will excuse Ramsay for murder, not you." He dropped his hand, releasing Tormod's fist. "Try to get along in the great hall, if you please. There are too many witnesses about. We need to be watching others, not creating a ruckus so we're the center of attention."

Art stood not far from them, a wide grin on his face.

That's what made him realize Coll was right. Tormod said through clenched teeth, "Fine. I'll do as you request, Coll, but only because you ask. Art needs to mind his words." He left the two of them to find his way to the hall, suddenly aware of the number of people in the surrounding area. The castle had been opened for a brief time so all could enjoy the festivities, and members of the burgh were flooding in through the gates.

The hell with Art. He would just keep a careful eye on Sorcha and Molly. He moved inside and waited in the passageway for Coll to arrive. Once he caught up with him, they stepped into the hall. "Busy place."

Coll said, "Aye. And are there not some beauties here this eve?" He scanned the hall as he spoke, but his eyes stopped when he caught something.

"What is it?" Tormod asked.

"I cannot believe what I'm seeing. It cannot be."

"What are you looking at?" Then he faltered, too. He knew exactly what Coll had seen.

"Do you see Molly?"

Aye, and his jaw had fallen open as soon as his eyes landed on her. "Aye, I see Molly."

"She does not look the same at all. I've not seen her in a gown before, only leggings." Coll crossed his arms, but then turned his attention to Sorcha. "Hellfire, would you not feast your eyes on Sorcha? She's a bronzed angel, I swear to the heavens."

Tormod could not take his gaze from Molly. While he had to admit she looked a bit uncomfortable in her attire, he could not take his eyes off her. Her lean, graceful body had caught his eye from the first, but he'd never seen her look as appealing as she did this eve. He'd never seen a lass as strong as Molly Ramsay either. A powerful archer like her mother, she was fierce and skilled. How he envied Molly.

While he fought to tear his gaze from her, two lads strode up to the lasses, clearly looking to score some kisses outside or something more. He narrowed his gaze as he watched one of the snakes do his best to charm the lasses, but apparently, neither one was interested. A few minutes later, the lad strode off as if a hound were nipping at his heels, and the lasses headed straight for them.

He almost felt sorry for Molly. Beautiful though she looked, she appeared to be about as comfortable as a brown trout basking on a cobblestone courtyard. Vowing to set her at ease, he smiled as they approached the ladies.

Up close, Molly was even more enchanting. Sorcha made some comment about her gown, but he was too distracted to make a comment, so he merely smiled at her and nodded, hoping she could read his approval from his expression.

Molly's sire showed up behind them, and after a short discussion on swordplay, he left. Sorcha and Coll chatted while Tormod did his best to come up with something to say to Molly. He did not have to think for long before he was shoved from behind, straight in Molly's direction. He almost knocked her over but caught her, and when he realized that his one hand had landed on her left breast, he saw fire. Spinning on his heel, he gave the perpetrator a wee shove. It was no surprise at all that it was Art.

Aye, he was a right bastard.

"Forgive me, Molly," he said, turning back to face her after he threw Art a scowl.

"You are forgiven. 'Twas an accident." She pulled her gaze from his, her face turning the color of the apples set out on the tables. She hurried away from him, back toward the dais where her parents sat, but Tormod followed her, grasping her arm to apologize again.

"Molly, please do not go. You look lovely tonight."

She turned to him and glowered. "Tormod, you need not resort to lies to make me feel better. I have already forgiven you. Please do not think on it again. But I know how I look in this gown, ridiculous. I pale in comparison to my sister. So do not attempt to placate me again." She reached up to massage her temple. "Forgive me, my head aches terribly. Please, I must go."

She turned away from him and he mumbled, "I was not lying. 'Tis the truth, you are lovely."

Frustrated, he crossed his arms as she approached her mother, holding her head. He'd not go over there with her parents nearby. Giving up, he returned to Sorcha and Coll.

"Is she ill?" Coll asked.

"She has a headache."

Sorcha said, "She gets them often. Mama will take her to her room, but I wish to relax and enjoy the entertainment tonight."

Shite. Was this not his luck that the one person he was interested in spending time with this eve was leaving? Hellfire, but he could barely take his eyes off the beauty.

But his interest in Molly also put him on his guard. It made him remember how dangerous it was to trust someone.

Many years ago, Tormod's elder brother, Lyall, had played an evil trick on him. His sire had never bothered to make a secret of his preference for Lyall. Tormod had been too small as a laddie, too sensitive. Or so his sire had liked to tell him.

In those lonely years, Tormod used to dream about what life would have been like had his mama not died when he was five summers. His sire had kept one of her favorite blue gowns, and every time Tormod opened the trunk it was kept in for something else, he used to lift the gown out. Even after so much time, it still held the aroma of flowers that reminded him of his mother.

His brother had seen him do it one day and teased him mercilessly.

Shortly after Lyall had married and Tormod had reached adulthood, his brother had offered to help him find his first woman. Desperate to lose his virginity, he had actually been fool enough to accept Lyall's help. His brother had promised to find an experienced woman for him—one who would teach him everything about the act. The night was arranged, and Lyall had gone so far as to lie to their sire to get Tormod out of doing his usual chores.

Tormod had bathed and dressed carefully that night before walking over to the hut Lyall had told him to visit. Once he arrived, he was surprised to see his brother there, having an ale with a couple of his friends, but no one said anything about what was about to take place.

What happened next haunted him still.

His brother pulled him aside, pointed him to a chamber, and then patted his back and pushed him onward. After taking a deep breath, he opened the door to the chamber, surprised to find it dark. He couldn't see the woman on the bed, but sensed she was there. He lit a candle, mostly because he wished to see what the lass looked like. Once he stepped near the bed, the covers were flung back at the same time as the chamber door popped open. His brother and his friends stood behind him hooting and hollering at the same time the lass jumped out of the bed shouting, "Here I am, Tormod. I'm the woman of your dreams."

It was his brother's wife dressed in his mother's blue gown. She laughed harder than any of the men in the chamber.

Horrified beyond belief, he raced out of the hut. If only he could have escaped the story as easily. His own brother had humiliated him, and his sister-in-law had helped. The tale had spread far and wide, and he'd been teased for months. It wasn't until he'd grown so much as to tower over his brother that the constant tormenting had finally stopped.

Over the next year or two, he'd sprouted like a wild weed, growing taller than his brother, and he'd had willing lasses since. But he'd sworn to himself he'd never trust anyone other than himself.

If you trusted people and gave them your heart, they would only rip it out and stomp on it.

* * *

Molly sat on the bench with her hand on her temple. This headache was worse than any of the others. She wished to lay her head on the table and sob, but she could not do so in front of all these people. Her gaze found her mother. Gwyneth had gone to tell Logan that she would escort Molly upstairs to her room, the only salvation she had when she was suffering this kind of attack.

Molly scanned the hall briefly to see if anyone was paying her any mind, but no one seemed to notice what she was going through. Hellfire, there was one lad staring at her from across the chamber, his gaze alone making her uncomfortable, but she could do naught but ignore him. Pivoting her head, she searched for her mother, but Gwyneth had been stopped by the king, so she wouldn't be returning quickly.

The pain in her head increased, making her feel as though the left side of her head was about to explode. Her next thought was that she was about to heave, something that happened occasionally when she had headaches this severe. Unable to wait for her mother, she headed toward the doorway, hoping she could get outside and toss her dinner into the bushes before she was seen by anyone.

Her stomach rumbled, inverted, and then bounced around like her cousin Lily in a field of flowers, and the searing pain in her head felt as though it branded her. Now that she'd found her way to the passageway, she moved toward the front door, closing her eyes whenever possible to help stay the incessant throbbing. Her mother's voice called to her from inside the hall, and she mumbled a slight, "Here, Mama."

When she was almost to the doorway, a hand shoved at her back. She arched in surprise, her eyes flying open to see who had grabbed her, but she was held in a vise-like grip that prevented her from turning. Pain shot through her body, and she fought another wave of nausea. She had no idea who stood behind her, and she had little strength to stop him.

A male voice whispered in her ear, "Scream and I'll kill you and then your mother."

She said naught as he shoved her down a dark passageway. Her hand managed to find his and dig into his skin, but he swung his fist into the middle of her back, hard enough to send more pain rippling through her.

"Stop. My message 'twill only take a moment." She didn't recognize his voice, but there was no mistaking it was full of animosity.

She fought him against his advice, pinching and kicking and scratching, but to no avail. He finally knocked her down to the ground, face first, and pinned her with his body.

"Now you listen, you wee bitch. You tell your sire, your cousin, and your uncle that we are coming for you and yours. You'll not know who we're after until the time is too late. 'Tis time for sweet revenge for all you've done to us. I'll not take you yet because I need you to deliver our message. Tell your sire we are ready to do battle. Retribution is coming."

She struggled underneath him but to no avail.

"Just know that judgment time is here. The Ramsays will pay for their transgressions."

He released her as soon as he heard the echo of steps coming toward them from the main corridor. Molly's attacker ran in the opposite direction as another male voice reached her ears. "Molly? Where are you?"

The passageway was still dark, and she could not determine who had called her name, but she answered because she thought the voice was familiar. "Here. I'm here on the floor." She rolled onto her back with a loud groan, the pain from the fist she'd taken spreading to the rest of her body.

Someone knelt beside her and reached down to grip her hand. "Molly? What happened?"

"Tormod? Please do not leave me. He attacked me, he punched me, he…my head…my back…"

"Shush. I'll stay with you." His gaze searched the area. "I believe he's gone. Who was it? Did you recognize him?"

"Nay, but please get me away from here. Please? Take me to my chamber. You can use this back staircase." She sat up and attempted to stand, but Tormod scooped her into his arms and ran down the passageway to the staircase, tearing up the steps as if his feet had been set afire.

"Tormod, be careful. I'm heavy, do not drop me."

He snorted. "You weigh about as much as my wee niece. Do not worry." When he reached the next floor, he scanned both directions before moving into the corridor. "Which way?"

She pointed in the direction of her chamber and he carried her inside and settled her on the bed. "You are hale? Would you like me to get your mother?"

"Nay, please do not leave me yet." She rolled onto her side, cuddling into a ball in an attempt to stop the pain.

Tormod lit two more candles, and he was going for a third when she shouted at him. "No more, please. 'Tis too painful for my head."

He knelt by her side and whispered to her, "Tell me what do to. How can I be of assistance? I can see the pain you are in. Let me find your mother." He pushed up only to find himself tugged back down by Molly.

"Please. I know not if he will come back." Tears ran down her cheeks and she opened her eyes to look at Tormod. How she appreciated that *he* was the one who'd come along. "My thanks. If you had not found me when you did, I do not know what would have happened." She could feel her face contort from the burst of pain that shot through her head.

His hand brushed her hair back from her face. "Is it your head? It pains you this much?"

"Aye," she said through clenched teeth. "And my back where he punched me. Did you see him?"

He held her hands, cocooning them with his heat. "Aye, but I did not get a good enough look to identify him, and I was too worried about you to follow him on foot."

The door burst open and Molly's sire flew into the chamber. He took one look at Tormod before grabbing him by the shoulders and heaving him against the far wall. As Tormod landed with a thud, Logan bellowed, "I'll kill you!"

"Nay, Papa! He saved me. Do not hurt him." Molly's hand flew up toward her sire, but the motion jarred her head and made her dizzy.

Her father stood by her bed, staring at Tormod as he scrambled to his feet, his arms held out in front of him as if he were pleading with a raging bull. "I promise naught happened. I have a great amount of respect for your daughter. I would never hurt her."

Her sire glowered at him.

"Papa, please." Tears covered Molly's cheeks. She tried to sit up on the bed, but the pain was too much and she collapsed backward. The door opened, and her mother and Sorcha came rushing in.

"Oh my. Logan, tell me what happened." Gwyneth sat on the side of the bed and reached for her daughter's hand. "Molly? How did you get here? Your head?"

Tormod said, "Allow me to explain, please. After Molly left the hall, I saw a man get up and follow her, so I decided to shadow them to make sure she was safe. When I entered the main passageway, they were nowhere to be seen. I stepped outside the main door to the courtyard, but she was not there either, so I moved back inside and checked the nearby passageways. When I found her, her attacker was running away."

"Who the hell was it? Who dared to touch my daughter?" Her father's voice was surely loud enough to be heard at the Grant keep.

Molly's mother tugged on his plaid. "Logan, her head. You're causing her more pain."

He leaned down and kissed Molly's forehead. "Forgive me, lass. Who was it? Who hurt you?" he whispered.

"I do not know. He came at me from behind. I think he ran off when he heard Tormod coming."

Her mother said, "You have our gratitude, Tormod." Logan grasped Tormod's shoulder in a motion that was as much an apology as Molly thought he'd get from her sire.

Gwyneth returned her attention to her daughter. "What did he want?"

"He had a message for me, actually a message for all the Ramsays."

"And what was that?" her sire asked.

"He said to tell you that they're coming for the Ramsays. 'Tis about revenge for something we've done to them. Sweet revenge, he said."

Dead silence settled in the chamber, and Molly rested her head back on the pillow and closed her eyes.

"Oh, Papa? He said to tell my sire, my cousin, and my uncle. Which cousin? He said they were ready for battle."

Logan knelt down so his gaze was level with his daughter's. "Molly, listen carefully. Do you think there is any chance the man who attacked you was Ranulf MacNiven? If so, the cousin he referred to is Torrian. Answer this one last question and I'll leave you to rest."

"Nay. I do not think I've ever seen this man before."

Logan stood and said, "Gwynie, you and Sorcha stay here. Tormod? Come with me. We have work to do."

CHAPTER THREE

TORMOD FOLLOWED LOGAN RAMSAY DOWN the staircase, rubbing his shoulder where he'd hit the wall. Shite, but the man was still a bull, amazing because he was no longer in his prime. Tormod would be wise to learn all he could from him.

"My lord? Where are we headed?" Tormod had to rush to keep up with him.

"You go outside and locate the rest of our team. I need to speak to the king and find a chamber where we can speak privately. Wait for us in the passageway. This cannot wait. I hope you've eaten."

"Nay, I have not, but pay it no mind. I'll survive."

Once they made it to the main passageway, Tormod hurried through the crowd toward the front entranceway. Scanning the area, he found Jamie and Braden conversing with three guards by the gate. Floods of people were still making their way inside, anxious to obtain the free food offered by the king once a moon. Word traveled through the burgh quickly whenever the king opened his gates.

He raced to Jamie's side, nodded to the guards and said, "We need to talk."

The Grant guards stepped away from the king's men, and Jamie pointed to a spot off to the side of the courtyard. Once they were far enough away not to be overheard, he asked, "What is it?"

"Molly was attacked. Logan wants the team to meet inside."

Braden's eyes widened. "Attacked? Someone dared to attack Uncle Logan's daughter?" Tormod had to agree that he could not believe someone had dared to do such a thing in the same building as her sire. Whoever the lad was, he had ballocks the size of boulders.

Just then, several guards came bellowing out of the castle. It was no surprise to Tormod when the men shouted, "No more allowed in. Those of you here, move out. The feast is over for this night. All are to leave the premises."

Jamie and Braden and Tormod fell back to the periphery, watching all that passed them. The guards ushered people out of the castle, saying, "Another day. The king will repay another day. Illness inside. Take your leave."

"This is Logan's doing," Tormod whispered. "Someone pushed Molly into a passageway and held her down to deliver a message to her sire and the rest of the Ramsays."

"What?" Jamie's expression did not hide his astonishment. "What in hell was the message?"

"He said they were ready to attack the Ramsays, and to be prepared for battle."

"God's bones! I cannot believe it happened while we were out here," Braden said.

"Check everyone who passes. See if you see aught suspicious," Tormod advised. "Once it slows, we'll go inside. In fact, let's move apart."

"How long ago was the attack?" Jamie asked as he drew his hand through his hair.

"Not long. A quarter of an hour maybe?"

As Braden stepped away from them, he turned and said, "My guess is the attacker is gone."

"I will not disagree with you, but 'twill not hurt to look." Oh, how Tormod wished to find the bastard. True, if he found the man who'd dared to touch Molly Ramsay, his status would raise, especially in the eyes of Logan Ramsay and King Alexander. But something else was driving him, too—he'd not forgotten how Molly had felt in his arms. He would gladly tear the man apart piece by piece for hurting the poor lass. The bastard had punched her in the back, the kind of punch that many considered out of line in hand-to-hand fighting in the lists. He vowed to do aught he could to protect her and erase that look of pain on her face. Cruelty was something he could not stomach.

The three moved to separate areas in the courtyard while the crowd continued to shift out of the castle, some pushing and shoving with such rudeness it was a wonder no one was hurt.

Tormod looked everyone over carefully, but he did not see anyone who reminded him of the man running down the passageway. He'd pulled up the hood of his dark mantle as he left the corridor. Few people had mantles on—most were clutching plaids and scarves to protect themselves from the chill of the night.

As soon as the crowd thinned, Tormod headed to the door, motioning for Braden and Jamie to follow. He met Coll in the corridor, and his friend led them to the smaller chamber Logan had found for the meeting. Art had apparently disappeared.

Once inside, they all settled into chairs, Art joining them at the last minute. Logan said, "My clan and family have been threatened." He repeated all he'd heard from Molly, then gave his thoughts as to their next steps. "I believe we have no alternative but to head home. Molly is having horrific headaches, and we have often found her symptoms coincide with attacks on our clan or the Grants. I know this does not make sense, but 'tis the truth.

"We were brought here to search out the MacNiven, and he has not been seen yet. With the problems Molly is dealing with, and the threat against my clan, I would be remiss to keep my family here. I'll discuss this with King Alexander before making my plans for certes, and he may request a team stay here and continue the search, but we need to reexamine our plan. I'll update you when we have made a decision."

Jamie said, "But there are more guards here. This could be the safest place for you. How many do you have to travel with you back to Ramsay land?"

"Mayhap a dozen. We'll make it. I have the two best archers in the land traveling with me, my wife and Molly. Sorcha is also strong."

"Mayhap we should travel with you." Jamie glanced at Braden and the rest of his team to gauge their reaction.

"That choice is yours, lads, but your assistance would be most welcome. Mayhap the man who attacked my daughter plans to attack us on the road, where we'll be more vulnerable. But I believe this could be tied to MacNiven, as he is the most obvious person to have revenge against the three people mentioned. He's escaped enough times that he knows his luck is running out, so he's going on the offensive instead of the defensive. He's planning to battle, and I think he'll head to Ramsay land. There are too many to fight in Edinburgh with the king's guards. True, *we* may be safer here, but I need to let my clan know of the threat made against us. I think his reason for telling Molly is something different."

"What reason?" Tormod asked.

"Because some of the members of the clan he plans to target are not here with us. He wants us together. He does not have enough men to attack in two places."

Jamie explained to Tormod and Coll, "Torrian and Uncle Quade, among others. Mayhap Torrian's wife, Heather."

"Aye, 'tis most logical, but why give him what he wants?" Tormod asked.

"Because together, we are invincible. We shall put an end to this gladly, and 'twill be even better if we can do it on our land." Logan began to pace the small chamber. "I'd leave now, but I do not wish to start in the dark, and Molly is not in any condition to travel. Hopefully, she'll improve overnight, as I need her firing arm. I plan to leave at dawn on the morrow, and I welcome anyone who wishes to travel with us."

"I'll travel with you." Jamie glanced at Braden. "And I'm hoping the others will join me."

Braden and Coll said, "Aye," in unison.

"Aye," Tormod said, "'twould be my honor to escort your family."

Logan nodded to him and then narrowed his gaze at Art, who lifted his chin as he considered his options.

"I'm not interested in traveling to Ramsay land or back to Grant land. I've decided to make Edinburgh my new home."

Logan took a step closer to him so he could look him in the eye. "And I trust you shall ferret out any information you can about the threat to the Ramsays, and you will send a messenger to me if you hear aught."

Art said, "I'll consider it."

Logan whispered, loud enough for all to hear, "I'll kill you with my bare hands if you learn aught and do not send it on to me. Understood?"

Art lost his haughty expression and swallowed hard. "Understood."

Logan spun on his heel and left the chamber.

Tormod's blood raced through his veins at the prospect of the new experience ahead of him. True, he did not favor working on a team—if growing up with Lyall and his father had taught him anything, it was that he could depend only on himself—but this assignment would give him the best of both worlds. The team was small enough that they'd have multiple opportunities to use their own skills to stand out, yet they would be able to help and support one another if need be.

He planned to make a name for himself so his brother would regret taunting him.

If not, he would not go home. He would no longer pretend to laugh along while his brother and father taunted him.

He'd had enough.

Molly jerked herself to a sitting position in the bed. She glanced around the chamber to try to place herself. Where was she? Her panting echoed through the chamber. The royal castle. She was still in their chamber in the royal castle. Her mother and Sorcha were asleep next to her.

She closed her eyes to force herself to recall what she'd been dreaming because something told her it was important. Who had she been dreaming about? She rubbed the sleep out of her eyes, but unfortunately, that did not help.

Suddenly, it all came back to her, and her hand shot to her throat. "Lord in heaven, please let it not be true!" She shook her head as if to deny the visions that filled her mind, but they persisted. The others needed to know.

Now.

"Mama, wake up." She shook her mother's shoulders until Gwyneth popped up on the bed.

"What is it?"

Sorcha groaned from the other side of the bed, covering her head with the pillow.

The door flew open and her sire stood in the doorway, awakened from his spot on the floor where he normally slept to keep watch on his family when they traveled. "What is it, Molly?"

"Ashlyn. I had a terrible dream about Ashlyn and Magnus. It was *that* kind of dream."

Her mother wrapped an arm around Molly's shoulder. "Take a deep breath and remember aught you can. Close your eyes, and tell us what you see."

This was her mother's tactic, and it usually worked. Her mother had the most amazing ability to calm her, slow her thoughts, and wrest memories from her that she had believed were long lost. She did as instructed while her sire pulled a stool over in front of her.

Her mother's soft voice carried to her. "Where are you?"

She took a deep breath and surveyed the area around her in the vision.

"Snow. I'm in the middle of a snowstorm. I cannot see because of the wind and the snow flurries all around me."

Her mother persisted. "Take your time and your view will improve. Tell me what you see."

She stood in the snow, lifting her chin to stare out over the landscape until she saw red. She jumped back, and her sire's voice came to her. "You must move forward, lass. Tell us what you see."

She tucked her arms close to her body for protection. "Blood. I see blood. Red snow everywhere."

"Look for the source. Whose blood is it? Go toward the blood. You'll not get hurt." Her father's hands rubbed down her arms.

She took two steps forward toward the red patch of snow. There was a darkness to it that spoke of a serious wound. She pulled back, not wanting to go near it.

"Nay. You must go forward," her mama whispered.

She persisted until she saw a man on the ground. She leaned down to identify him. "Magnus. Magnus is bleeding from his leg. And Ashlyn is up on the wall. There are men everywhere. One is bellowing because he has an arrow in his shoulder."

"Go on…"

"He is the leader. He tells them to follow him. They leave and Ashlyn gets down, but she cannot reach Magnus in time." Her eyes flew open, and her knuckles went to her face, rubbing, as if she could rid herself of the vision.

Her father grabbed her shoulders and leaned over to kiss her forehead. "Well done, Molly."

"But what does it mean? Magnus cannot be dead?"

"It could mean many things," her mother replied, "but I do believe they are in danger. We must go after them." Molly's parents exchanged a glance, and Molly could tell by the look on her sire's face that he agreed. "We must," Gwyneth continued. "You were correct about Ashlyn being in trouble before."

"You mean the dream that sent Da to check on the team in the Highlands?"

"Aye, but last time you only saw a lass thrown across a horse. Your dreams are becoming clearer. This time, you *knew* it was Ashlyn."

"What does that mean?"

Her mother rubbed her back. "I think your skills as a seer are becoming stronger."

"Why? Mayhap I do not want them to be stronger." She rubbed the sweat from her palms onto the bedding.

"Daughter," Gwyneth said gently, "this is a God-given gift. You must accept it. We are proud you've been chosen." She turned to Molly's sire, who was standing by the door. "Go, Logan. See what our king says."

"Dawn is almost here." He opened the door and turned to them before stepping into the passageway. "I'll find you something to break your fast, then I'll search out the king and Jamie. We must change our plans." She peered up at her mother, waiting to see what she would say after he left.

"How is your head?" Gwyneth asked softly.

"The pain is easing. 'Tis much better."

"You needed to get this message out."

"Do you believe it is true, Mama?"

"I am not sure of the details. I believe you are telling me what you saw, but they may not all be true. But we must go after them. We should not have allowed them to make such a trip alone."

"What about Sorcha and me?"

She patted her hands on her lap. "Your sire and I will head to Grant land to help Ashlyn and Magnus, but you and Sorcha are going home. 'Tis best for you to be on Ramsay land with all our warriors. 'Tis always best to be on land we know. Edinburgh is uncertain, even though the royal guards are here, they have many tasks to focus on. The king is a busy man. We shall send plenty of guards to escort you." She helped her daughter back onto the bed. "Rest your head for a few moments more. Close your eyes. You will probably have a long journey today."

Molly closed her eyes, praying that her visions were wrong.

CHAPTER FOUR

TORMOD SAT IN THE SMALL chamber, the same one they'd used the night before. Word had reached him that plans had changed, so he'd rushed in to hear what had transpired overnight.

Logan stood at the head of the table. He waited for the servants to deliver bread, cheese, and porridge to the men. Once they had left and the doors were closed, he began. "This may come as a surprise to many of you, but we have come to believe that our daughter Molly is a seer. Gwynie and I adopted her from an Englishman, and we do not know her family's history. My sister Avelina has the same tendencies, so I know how valuable the skill of prophecy can be. Molly is still new to her talent, so we are not certain how much of what she sees will come to pass, but she has been right often enough for us to act upon her pre-dictions."

A heavy feeling dropped into Tormod's belly, a coldness that he often felt when he heard stories about the unknown. Molly was a seer. How did one handle such a gift? He hoped he would have the opportunity to ask her more about this new talent of hers. Some people swore by the ability of seers. He forced himself to focus back on Logan.

"Molly has told us that Magnus and Ashlyn are in trouble, so we have changed our plans. Gwyneth and I will take a couple of guards and head toward Grant land in the hopes of meeting up with Magnus and Ashlyn along the trail. The rest of you are to escort our daughters home. I want them on Ramsay land as soon as possible. The king is sending twenty guards with you. Jamie and Braden, you are in charge of the journey, and I will speak to both of you about the trail I'd like you to take.

"Tormod, I am assigning you to specifically watch over Molly. You are the one who felt the need to follow her when she was kidnapped, so it would seem the heavens have already given you that task. Coll, I am assigning you to specifically protect Sorcha. They are both strong archers, but I especially worry about Molly on this journey. I do not know if her headaches will return. If they do, she may not be capable of riding, in which case she's to ride with you, Tormod. I do not want either of my daughters in the front, so Jamie and Braden will be in the lead. I want to keep it as quiet as possible that the lasses ride with you. We have no idea what you may encounter on the way to Ramsay land." He swept his gaze over each of the men at the table.

Tormod squared his shoulders. Molly's safety was entirely his responsibility, and he welcomed this opportunity to prove himself. He was most grateful he'd been assigned this task, thanking the heavens that he'd not have to watch another with her. She had a pull on him that he didn't understand.

"Any questions?"

Jamie asked, "What are your plans once you locate Ashlyn and Magnus? What would you like me to tell your brother and your laird, Torrian?"

"We will not know that until we see how they are. If Molly's dream is accurate, we will have to escort them onto Grant land. She saw Magnus seriously injured. She also saw a dark force attacking them, though she could not identify it." His gaze searched their faces at the table. "And none of you are to ask her about her visions. Understood? I have given you all the information you need to know. If she has any more dreams or headaches, Jamie and Tormod will handle the discussion of them."

Tormod nodded, the significance of the situation finally settling on him. If anything happened to Molly, he'd be answering to Logan and Gwyneth Ramsay. He wiped the sweat off his brow, hoping his hands did not betray the tremors in his body. With any luck, it would be an uneventful trip.

"I'll speak to Tormod and Jamie at more length outside. The rest of you prepare for a long, hard journey. You will travel through the night until you reach Ramsay land."

Tormod climbed out of his chair and followed Jamie and Logan into the castle courtyard, away from prying ears. He had no idea what he was about to hear, but he'd do his best to make his laird proud. He wondered what his sire and his brother would think of this assignment. They'd find some way to make it appear inconsequential, as always.

They'd be wrong. He knew this was the most important job he'd ever been assigned.

Logan came to a stop in the courtyard, glanced around to make sure they were alone, and then said, "Tormod, I'm trusting you with my daughter's life. Please do not take it lightly."

"Nay, my lord." Why had his voice come out in a squeak?

"Now, I'm telling you both, do not allow anyone to question her about her dreams. They pain her terribly. If her headaches continue, and she needs to ride with you, I'll remind you to be on your best behavior at all times, Tormod. Molly and Sorcha will advise me of any untoward advances made by any of your guards. Your job is to protect them from the other lads, as well, though I do not expect aught to happen. Art has wisely chosen to stay here, and he was the only warrior I ever doubted."

"I would never disrespect your daughters," Tormod said. "I'll do my verra best to protect Molly."

"Jamie, get them home as fast as you can without overdoing it."

Jamie rubbed his jaw before he crossed his arms in front of him. He was not quite as broad as his brother Jake, and he'd never had the presence of his older twin, who'd been a natural born leader from a young age, but Jamie was changing. Tormod liked working with him and trusted his judgment. "May I ask your opinion?" Jamie finally asked. "Do you consider the two issues to be related? What exactly will we find outside the burgh?"

Logan tipped his head to the side as he stared up at the sky, choosing his words apparently. "Aye, I believe these two incidents to be related. MacNiven wishes to end this battle. He's a hunted man, and there are only two options left to him if he wishes to escape the hanging he's due. Mayhap he plans on traveling to the East or somewhere he cannot be reached. He has the coin to arrange such a journey, but he's demented enough to require repayment for all the injustices he feels we've done to him. The second possibility is that he hopes to hold someone for ransom. His life for theirs. Either way, he's been causing trouble for our clan and the Grants for long enough, and we'll not run from a confrontation. Since you have chosen to go along with us, you may find yourself doing battle with him once I get my daughters on safe ground. I could not have chosen finer guards to go and protect my lasses. My thanks for volunteering to go with us."

"What about your wife?" Tormod asked. "Are you not worried about her? Only a fool would doubt her archery, but with only two of you, she could be at risk."

Logan snorted. "MacNiven's afraid of Gwynie. Everyone is. She can handle herself. In fact, I thought hard about sending Gwynie with you and heading north on my own with a few guards, but I'm expecting that we shall find trouble, and I'd prefer to have her by my side. We do best when we guard each other. We've worked together for many, many years. She can anticipate my actions and I, hers. Do not forget that my daughters are both skilled archers if you find yourselves under attack. Send them into the trees."

"I'll not forget their skills," Jamie replied, nodding. "They can both outshoot me in the archery field. Do not worry, Uncle. We shall protect your daughters. When will they be ready to leave?"

"We have no time to waste. I'd like you on your way by the mid-morn. We'll leave directly after you. The king's cook will provide you with plenty of food to take along. Inform your men, Jamie, and I'll speak to the Ramsay guards."

———◆———○———◆———

Molly donned her leggings and tunic, topped off with a wool plaid to keep her warm. When she rode, she also wore a mantle, but if she had to shoot, she dropped it and counted on the plaid to keep her warm. It was the best way to keep her arms free so she could shoot properly.

She moved down the stairs, leaving Sorcha behind to gather her belongings, as she always brought more than Molly did. Down in the great hall, she was pleased to see her mother speaking with the cook, gathering items for them to take along on their respective journeys. Her mother gave her a kiss on her cheek, but then continued to pack two bags—one for her trip, and one for Molly's group.

"How is your head, my sweet?"

"Much better. The potion helped."

"Good. I'll send a small sack of the powder with you. Your sire instructed your cousin to move quickly, so you'll not have much time to rest. That worries me."

"I'll be fine, Mama. I just wish to get home, so moving quickly will suit me."

"As long as your headaches stay away. If not, they could slow you down." She stuffed some bricks of cheese inside each satchel.

"I'll deal with it until we are on Ramsay soil."

"You must not slow until you are inside the gates. Do not trust anyone you meet along the way."

"I know, Mama."

Her mother grasped her shoulders. "Molly, I hope this does not make you uncomfortable, but we have assigned Tormod to protect you, and we have chosen Coll to protect Sorcha. Your father asked your cousins to lead because they have the training for it. You are as comfortable with Tormod as with any lad, are you not?"

She nodded, staring at the ground to hide her blushing cheeks, hating to discuss this with her mother. If her mother knew how she truly felt, she probably would not have assigned Tormod to protect her. Tormod made her feel strange, but she did not worry he would do anything inappropriate. She thought of the alternatives, of the other men going along. "I think he's best," she finally said. "I would argue with you about taking care of myself, but my back still pains me from the attack last night. If my headaches start, between the two problems, I may not be able to ride alone, especially if we are moving quickly." She hated to admit she needed a man's strength, but there was no denying it. She trusted Tormod more than many of the others.

Truthfully, she had to admit she wouldn't mind Tormod's arms around her at all.

Molly was eager to get away from Edinburgh for fear of another attack, and though she hated to part with her parents, she was also worried about Ashlyn and Magnus.

Less than an hour later, Molly and the others left the royal castle. She did her best to keep the tears from falling down her face. Ever since her parents had adopted her, she'd had a strange feeling whenever they separated, as if they'd forget about her and leave her behind, or never come back for her.

Or give her away like her true sire had done.

Her parents had insisted that would never happen, that she was a true part of their family. Yet the old fears still found their way to the forefront of her mind on her worst days. Her sole motivation was to make her adoptive parents proud of her—to give them a reason to keep her.

Sorcha had all the self-confidence Molly wished to have. She'd been pleased to hear Coll was assigned to protect her, so she hadn't minded leaving their parents. That was the norm for them—Sorcha was always interested in lads, Molly only sometimes.

Their journey was uneventful until around dusk. Molly started to have another headache, and the pain rippled through her, starting behind her eyes and shooting down to her toes. Hellfire, but she was not ready to deal with this again. She massaged her head with one hand while the other hung on tight to the reins.

Tormod appeared next to her immediately. "Your head pains you again?"

Molly could not lie, though she wished he would leave her be. "Aye. The pain has started again." Another stabbing sensation shot through her skull and she leaned forward, throwing her horse into a bit of a rant. "This time 'tis behind my eyes, impairing my vision." She tipped toward him without realizing it.

Tormod grabbed her horse's reins, leading the mare over to the side of the path.

"What are you doing?" She opened one eye to glare at him.

"I'm doing what I was instructed to do. You'll ride with me from here."

"Nay. 'Tis not so bad. I can ride alone, Tormod."

"I'm following your sire's instructions." He leaned over and lifted her off her horse, situating her in front of him on the saddle.

She was in too much pain to argue. Jamie appeared at their side. "Problems, cousin?"

Molly nodded. "Headaches again, but I can likely still ride alone. I do not need…"

"Nay, you will not ride alone. Tormod did as he was ordered to do. Trust him, Molly. Lean your head on him. Close your eyes and sleep. You must be overtired from your dream last night." He took the reins of her horse and handed them to one of the guards before returning to the front of the line of horses.

Too tired to argue, Molly glanced back at Tormod with a sheepish look on her face. Men. How they liked to bark orders expecting no argument. Still, she did not mind that she was on Tormod's horse, since she preferred him to the others. Would he allow her to lean her head on his shoulder as her cousin had suggested? She guessed it would be the only thing to ease her pain.

Tormod rubbed her arm. As if reading her thoughts, he said, "Jamie is correct. Lean your head back. 'Tis almost dark and we were instructed to ride through the night. You may as well try and sleep. How is your back where you were hit by the fool?"

"My thanks. It still pains me, too, but I'm trying not to think on it."

"Get in whatever position relieves your pain. I can handle you which-ever way you wish. You're light as a bunny riding in front of me."

She couldn't help but smile. "Hardly a bunny, but..." were the only words she managed to get out before her head fell back against his shoulder. She settled against him, easing back as gently as she could, a slow moan coming from her as she savored the warmth and comfort of leaning her head against his plaid. She had to admit he even carried a pleasing scent. He wrapped his arm around her middle as he tucked her close, but all she could do was lean against him and close her eyes.

She fell fast asleep.

Almost an hour had passed, and the lass continued to sleep. Tormod had originally thought it would be best if she slept through the night.

His opinion had changed. While he was desperate to protect her, every soft moan she made sent a surge of lust to his loins. The brush of the soft mounds of her breasts had tormented him from the moment she settled back against him. Hours had passed now, and from her slight changes in position here and there, he thought he knew exactly what size her breasts were. The perfect size in his mind. He'd spent the better part of the last hour trying to guess the color of her nipples. Would they be that dusky shade of coral or the rich brown color of her hair? It did not matter to him which one, he just wanted to know.

Hellfire, but the lass fit him perfectly. He'd been flooded with grati-tude on the long-ago day when he'd finally outstripped his brother in height, and now he'd found a new reason to be grateful. Molly's long, lean body, tucked perfectly against his.

Coll rode up next to him. "Molly's asleep?"

"Aye. She had one of her headaches again."

Coll waggled his eyebrow at Tormod. "Sorcha's asleep, too. Good thing, because she'd be asking me why there's something hard in my plaid." He chuckled so loudly, it was a marvel the lasses still slept.

Tormod sighed. Coll was a fool. "You best hope her sire does not hear you talk," he muttered, keeping his voice down so as not to wake the lasses.

"And how could he know?" Coll asked.

Tormod said, "You'd be surprised. Did you forget he's a spy for the Crown? I'd not take that for granted."

"You worry over much, lad," Coll said with a grin. "Take what you can when you can. 'Tis my belief."

"That's where you and I differ. I'll not disrespect a lass, especially not when she's asleep."

There was a pause, then Coll asked, "And you believe all that Molly says about her visions?"

"Aye, I do. You do not?"

"Nay," Coll said, speaking more softly now. "I believe 'tis something she invented for attention."

"I disagree. Molly would never do such a thing. She's a fighter." And why did he have this sudden urge to put a fist in the other man's face? Coll had been a better friend to him than many, but this was a side of him he didn't like.

"I do not believe in seers."

"So you do not believe the tales about her aunt, Avelina Ramsay, and the storm over the sapphire sword, the one that my sire said lit up the Highlands?"

"Nay, 'twas all created to stir the Scots' loyalty. I do not believe in the fae or the swords or naught."

Tormod shook his head, wondering how anyone could listen to Alex Grant, their chieftain, speak of the sight and think he'd been deceived. Nay, his laird was the mightiest in all the land, and if he believed it was true, so did Tormod. "I do. Alex Grant would not lie about such a thing. Even my sire said 'twas true. He was fighting as a Grant warrior at the time, heading toward Ramsay land when it happened. The storm was so fierce, it had the biggest and brawniest warriors crying like bairns in the night, he said."

"Such tales are sheer twattle. I'll not believe in that nonsense."

"Mayhap you'll learn different on this journey. I can see in her eyes how much pain her headaches cause her. Something powerful is behind them, you'll see."

Coll simply shrugged and took off ahead of them.

Tormod tugged Molly a bit closer and rested his chin on her head. "I believe you, lass."

Molly let out a deep sigh in her sleep and clutched his plaid.

CHAPTER FIVE

W HEN MOLLY AWAKENED, THEY WERE on the edge of Ramsay land.

"We'll be there soon, lass. How is your head?" Tormod asked as he handed a skin of water to her.

She reached up to massage her temples, surprised it did not pain her to do so. "Better. 'Tis better." An hour later, a group of men on horses crossed the meadow to greet them. As they came closer, she recognized two of them as Torrian and Kyle Maule, his second. To her surprise, the others were her uncle Drew with two of his three sons, Tad and Tomag.

"Uncle Drew?" His horse headed straight for her.

"Aye, your aunt Lina has come to see you, Molly. Fear not, she will help you with your dreams."

She noticed Tormod flip his head around to nod at Coll, a smirk on his face, and wondered what that was about, but she was so pleased to be safely on Ramsay land that she quickly forgot about it.

Sitting straight up so as not to touch Tormod, she replied, "I cannot wait to see Aunt Lina, but how did she know, Uncle Drew?"

"She just did. I cannot tell you any more than that, lass. She'll explain when you see her."

They all rode to the keep together, and when Tormod helped her down from his horse, she had to grip him tight to keep from falling to the ground. Her knees buckled under her, something that did not usually happen. She'd been riding horses for ages now.

"Careful, lass. You've been asleep for a long time."

Her uncle Drew, who'd already dismounted, came up behind her.

Molly glanced from Tormod to Uncle Drew in confusion. "I have? It did not seem like verra long."

Uncle Drew patted her shoulder. "Those dreams can be exhausting. Your aunt will explain it all. Come, give your uncle a hug." Drew pulled her into his warm embrace, then nodded to Tormod. "Our thanks for keeping Molly safe."

Tormod nodded. "My honor as a Grant warrior, my lord."

Molly swung around to look at him. "Many thanks, Tormod." She could feel the blush climb from her neck to her cheeks, so she turned around to greet the others from her clan before hurrying in to the keep, her long limbs rushing her along.

After they all exchanged greetings with Molly's kin, Torrian and Uncle Quade hastened the Grant guards, Molly, and Uncle Drew and Aunt Avelina into the solar. Sorcha had gone off to seek out her sisters.

"We welcome those from the Grant clan," Torrian said from behind his desk, "and you may stay as long as you like, but we are puzzled by your quick return. Were you not seeking Ranulf MacNiven, last seen deep in the Highlands?"

Jamie filled them in on the attack on Molly, the warning she had received, and her vision.

Uncle Quade asked, "So Logan and Gwyneth departed Edinburgh in search of Ashlyn and Magnus without knowing their location?"

"Aye," Jamie replied. "They left based on what Molly had seen in her vision. Uncle Logan also asked me to share his belief about what is to come."

"Go ahead," Torrian nodded toward him. "We are anxious to hear."

"Since MacNiven's identity has been uncovered, he is searching for a way to escape his hanging." Jamie allowed that to settle before he continued. Then he shared Uncle Logan's interpretation of the situation—that either MacNiven would try to wreak revenge and then run, or he'd try to kidnap one of the Ramsays to bribe his way out of an execution order.

Torrian glanced at his sire. "What do you think, Papa? Do you agree?"

"Aye, those are two possibilities. Drew? What think you on this matter?"

Drew Menzie rubbed his hands together before he spoke. "I know naught about MacNiven, but the most reasonable possibility is that he will try to reason his way out of the hangman's noose, especially knowing how angry the king was over his escape. His sneaky method got him away once, but it will not happen again. If MacNiven is the cause of Lina and Molly's dreams, then I'd guess he'll try to kidnap someone. 'Tis definitely the way of his people. He'd have no misgivings about it."

Torrian asked, "Molly, the visions are still new for you, are they not? Did Uncle Logan believe they would need to travel all the way to Grant land to help Magnus and Ashlyn?"

Molly replied, "Aye. There was a storm recently, so he's guessing he and Mama will have to get them back to their clan before they can return here. But he will leave as soon as possible. He wants MacNiven."

"Molly, have you had other dreams about storms while you were gone, something you could share with us?" Uncle Quade asked.

"Aye. At the time, I was not sure that it was a prediction. I saw two forces moving together, two dark forces, and they created a cloud that seemed to cover all the land. 'Tis difficult to explain."

"Aye, and I know this is all new to you." Her uncle, who was sitting at a desk exactly like his son's, turned to face his only sister. "Avelina, please share your vision with them."

"Of course." Aunt Lina cleared her throat and stood in front of the group. "As you know, I had predicted there would be peace for the Highlands for two decades. Darkness has now returned. A battle is coming, and I do not yet know how difficult 'twill be. Molly has seen it, and I have seen it, too. We must be vigilant and plan for this, not be caught unawares."

"How did you know to come here?" Jamie asked. "Did you receive a message from Uncle Logan?"

"Nay," Aunt Lina said. "I'm here because I saw Molly's troubles, and because I saw the darkness return. I promised Quade and Logan I would let them know as soon as I had a vision indicating a change. It happened three nights ago. Molly came to me in a vision two nights ago. Drew and I felt it best for us to come at once so we could be together, and I wished to talk with Molly."

Braden added, "Uncle Logan said the same. He thought it best if the Ramsays were all together. We're easier targets divided."

Uncle Drew asked, "So what do we do? Micheil and Diana are away, so we cannot expect them to travel here, and I agree we are best here together."

Torrian said, "We prepare for battle, and we wait for Uncle Logan's return, see if he has learned anything new."

Uncle Quade cracked his knuckles, something Molly had only seen him do when he was worried. "Until then, we'll keep our gates closed to all except family. Mayhap Molly or Avelina will have more dreams to guide us."

"Naught is more important than practice," Jamie said. "You need everyone in the lists, and we should arrange for an archery field inside the bailey for target practice. Molly needs to stay inside."

Molly had never experienced such tension before now, and worse, it was emanating from everyone. Her gaze moved from face to face, searching for a smile—even a hint of one—but found naught.

Torrian said it best. "War is coming."

"And we shall be ready," Jamie added. They dispersed after that, but it did nothing to dispel the heavy cloud Molly felt hanging overhead. Her spirits lifted when she saw her sister Maggie awaiting her outside of the solar.

"Molly, they say you've been hurt," she said, running over. "Are you hale and hearty?"

Her sister's sweet concern warmed her heart. How she loved Maggie, who'd been by her side ever since their sire had sold them off. Maggie had taken it very hard, but she was happy and at peace on Ramsay land. At four and twenty, she was content to stay with their clan, and like Molly, had never mentioned a wish to settle down.

"I was only hurt a bit. The man punched me in my back, and 'tis quite sore, but 'tis improving. Do not worry about me."

Maggie hugged her. "Am I hurting your back? Forgive me if I do, but I must hug you, for I was so worried all the while you were gone, and then I heard you were hurt..."

"Nay, you're not hurting my back."

Maggie whispered, "Promise me you'll never leave me. I wish you would not travel as an archer or with Mama and Papa on their spying missions. 'Tis too dangerous."

Molly swiped the tears away forming at the corners of her sister's eyes. "I promise. But I cannot promise I'll never travel, just know I'll always come home."

A sudden flash of darkness crossed her mind when she said those two words, and she stumbled.

"What is it, Molly?" her sister screeched.

"Naught. 'Tis naught, Maggie. I am just tired." She forced herself to straighten, though her body willed her to collapse onto a bed.

How she wished it to be the truth. Lord, but she was suddenly frightened.

Tormod sat at a trestle table a distance away from the dais and the Ramsay family. His gaze rarely left Molly. He hadn't known her before this journey, but each time he saw or spoke to the lass, he was more entranced by her. She lacked the kind of voluptuous curves that drove most men wild, but her beauty was classic, and she carried herself like royalty. Her posture was perfect, and she held her head high with a sense of confidence.

The fact that she was one of the most skilled archers in the land only made her more enticing. Some lads would argue with him, but Tormod wished for nothing less than a strong female. His brother's wife was an example of what he did not want—a simpering, controlling woman who was only interested in her own gains.

Many of the warriors left for the lists, but Tormod chose to wait for the archery lessons that Molly, her brother, Gavin, and Quade's youngest son, Gregor, had promised to give to anyone who was interested. He was eager to learn from Molly and watch her shoot, and he'd heard about Gavin and Gregor's prowess at Castle Dubh, where they'd last faced MacNiven. Torrian had already sent a group out to set up the targets, and while Tormod knew he probably should have gone to help, he could not tear his gaze from Molly.

He chased after Molly when she left the great hall. "May I go with you, lass? Would you mind giving me some pointers on my archery skills?"

She spun around as if she'd just noticed him standing there. "Of course, I enjoy teaching archery."

"I know 'twill be difficult because we are required to be inside the curtain wall, but I'm sure I can still learn much from you and your brother and cousin."

"Torrian could not find a satisfactory distance inside the gates, so he convinced Uncle Quade to send guards out while we shoot at the archery field. Accuracy can only be guaranteed when you practice at long distances." She pointed as the guards opened the gates at their approach. "'Tis not far. You need not mount."

Tormod, pleased with this development, if only because it meant he got to walk alongside Molly. There were others about them, also moving toward the field for lessons, but his senses were all fixed on her. "How long have you been practicing archery?"

"I started shortly after we were adopted by Mama and Papa. I was around eleven summers."

"Your sire mentioned that in Edinburgh. I had not been aware of it before." Tormod had been stunned to learn she was not a Ramsay by blood. He'd figured she and Sorcha had earned their skills with the bow from their parents.

"Probably because we do not speak of it much. I do my best not to recall anything about my life before joining the Ramsays. I swore I'd never leave the clan."

"Yet you did to go to Edinburgh," Tormod mentioned.

"Aye, but only because I was with my parents. I enjoy traveling with them."

"Of what age are you now?" Tormod could not begin to guess, though he thought she was past the usual Scottish marrying age, but younger than his seven and twenty.

"Seven and twenty."

He could not help but smile. "As am I. And you are not pledged to anyone? Being the laird's niece, I would think you would marry." Tormod could not believe he had asked the question—something he'd never asked a lass before, but he simply wished to know.

"Nay. I am not interested in marrying." They'd reached the field, and Molly chose her area of the field and found arrows to place in her quiver.

Tormod glanced at the others setting up to practice, but then turned his attention back to Molly. "Why not?" He stared at her, transfixed by the way she held herself, her confidence sending out an aura that drew him in. "Is that not the wish of all lasses?"

Her gaze lifted to his. "Not this lass. I have only one goal in life."

"And that is?" He could barely contain himself as he waited for her response.

"I wish to become as good an archer as my mother, and I intend to push myself until I have achieved that goal. Sorcha is good, and so is Ashlyn Grant, but I believe I can outdo them and gain the skills my mother has."

Tormod was unsure how to react to this since it was most unusual. Oh, he'd heard many lads say they wished to be the best swordsman in the land, but the best archer? Her mother had accomplished something so rare in their world. Could she possibly attain such a goal? "I hope you do not set yourself up for disappointment. 'Tis a lofty goal."

"Why? I wish to do as my mother has done."

Tormod did not know how to explain it, but thought he'd try. While achieving the same as one's parent was not an uncommon goal, her parents were indeed special. "Your mother is unlike most women in the Highlands. Not many tread in a man's steps as she does. But you have the gift of being taught by the best, so you could definitely achieve what your mother has done, especially if you train often on your land. I hear 'tis the best place to train."

He also was uncertain how to explain his goals were similar. He wished to be the best in the land at anything that would let his sire know that he had talent and was worthy of being a Grant warrior.

Molly stared at the gray clouds overhead, a far-away look on her face. "Mayhap a little more. I'd like to gain the skills to be able to travel alongside my mother. Now I travel with my parents so I can learn from her. Someday, I hope to be chosen for my own abilities, not because I am Gwyneth Ramsay's daughter, but because I am one of the best in the land. What think you would be a better goal? What is yours?"

Tormod scowled and set to work on his bow, trying to buy himself time to think of a good answer to her question. In truth, he didn't know how to answer, beyond that he wanted to prove himself to his family, especially to his sire. Ever since he could remember, his brother had bested him in everything they did, and the few times he'd been better than his brother, his father had come up with an excuse for the lad. His brother was overtired, overworked. The excuses had no end. But he did not want her to think less of him, to see him as the small, sad laddie he had been.

Molly set herself up in front of the target and pulled out her bow. He was drawn to watch her. This morn she was dressed in her usual outfit of leggings and a tunic, just like her mother often wore. He could see the muscles in her arms ripple and tense as she pushed them to their limit, pulling on the bow enough to send her arrow off to the farthest target. A loud thwack echoed across the meadow as her arrow hit the center of the target.

She turned to grin at him. "Is that satisfactory for you?"

"Aye, can you not teach me to shoot with that accuracy?" Damn, but the lass was good.

"Aye, I will give you lessons, but it takes serious practicing to improve your skills. Show me your stance. But first," she gave him a sly grin, "you must answer my question."

Tormod frowned, not wanting to say the words out loud, but he also did not wish to lie to her. "I've always wished to do better than my brother," he finally said. "My sire has always made it clear that he thinks 'twill never happen, which drove me for many years." He paused. "Suddenly, competition with my brother does not hold the appeal it used to hold for me." Perhaps that was not entirely truthful, yet something had happened to him when he'd been assigned as her protector. His priorities had changed. "I hope to make my laird proud, and be the best warrior I can be." In his own mind, he had to add that he wished to make his sire eat every one of his words—all the times he'd told him he could never measure up to Lyall's accomplishments. He'd like to gain their respect, but mayhap that was not even possible. They both lived in the past.

For the better part of an hour, Molly patiently worked with Tormod. Much as Tormod wished it were otherwise, she seemed to have no more interest in him than she did in any other lad on the field. But he learned from her. She knew much more than he did about archery and was a far better shot, no matter how he tried.

After they'd practiced together for a short time, something changed. He did not know what had caused the shift between them, but he could feel it. He'd done his best to hide his attraction to her, but when he set himself up for another shot, he felt her gaze on him. It was a *heated* gaze, and it traveled down his length and all the way back up again. He let his arrow fly and almost missed his target completely.

He stepped closer to her and watched her moisten her lips with her tantalizing tongue, knowing that she was oblivious to how the gesture tormented him, sending the blood through his body at twice the usual speed. Her gaze lifted to his, still heated, and he wished to lean over and taste her lips.

"Lass?" he whispered.

"Hmmm?" She stared at his lips.

"If you continue looking at me that way, you'll embarrass us both."

"What way?" she asked, jumping a little in shock.

He grinned and said, "The same way I'd like to look at you."

Jamie called his name, interrupting their small intimacy. He could tell by the dark shade of red crossing Molly's features that she was horrified, so he turned and stepped in front of her, hoping her cousin hadn't seen the blush in her cheeks.

Jamie joined them, the lads who had been practicing with their swords trailing behind him, and called the group together in the center of the field. "In view of what we have ahead of us, I'd like to train a bit differently today. Many of you have practiced your archery skills, some of you have worked on your swordsmanship, but I need you all to be agile and quick, so we will run daily until we receive word from Logan Ramsay."

Tormod chewed on his thumbnail. He wished for them to run? Surprised but willing, he glanced at the others for their reaction. Running was not something they usually did in the Grant lists. There, they practiced for strength and power, not speed. The best reaction came from Molly.

"Run? I love to run," she said. "Can we not make it a race, Jamie?"

Jamie got a gleam in his eye and glanced at the others. Besides Tormod and Molly, Sorcha, Coll, Gavin, Gregor, Braden, and a few more Ramsay guards were present. "You wish to make it a race? Individual or team, Molly?"

Coll and Braden yelled out as one, "Individual."

"You'll regret that, lads," Gavin said, a smirk spreading across his face.

"Nay," Coll said. "I wish to beat the lassies. 'Tis always fun to beat girls."

Gregor glanced at Gavin. "They'd like to beat the lassies, Gavin. 'Twill be fun." It was obvious he was barely holding back laughter.

"Aye," Gavin said. "We all say individual."

Tormod frowned, totally confused. "Why are the two of you so amused?"

Gavin said, "Just having fun. We'll all run."

Jamie used a rope to mark off the starting point, then gave them instructions on where to place certain rocks to mark the track. "Five times around the field for the first race. You must run to the outside of the four rocks."

Tormod glanced around the field. Shite, but he was making the lassies run a long distance. "Are you sure you do not want us to start out with two circles instead of five?"

Coll said, "Aye, we do not wish to show the lassies up too much. Five trips around the field is too much for a soft lass." He winked at Sorcha, who grinned in response. There was something saucy about her look that reminded Tormod of the amusement of her brother and cousin. What were they about?

"Nay, I'm sure they'll finish," Tormod added. In truth, he wasn't, but

Coll's attitude chafed.

"The race stands as I first announced," Jamie replied. "Five trips around. First one back to this line wins. Everyone runs. Find your place, and when my arm drops, you go. Any questions?"

They all lined up—Coll, Sorcha, Gavin, Gregor, Braden, Molly, Tormod, plus three of the Ramsay guards. Tormod kept his focus on Jamie, whom he knew to be fast. He vowed to beat the other lads, so he would push himself to impress Molly.

Jamie's arm dropped and they charged ahead. Tormod watched his opponents, noticing they all kept about the same pace through the first circle. He had to admit he was proud of Molly and Sorcha. They'd both been able to stay with the lads. They headed into the second lap and Tormod smiled as he noticed Coll falling back a bit, along with one of the guards. This would be easy.

As he started the third lap, he was surprised to notice both Molly and Sorcha were still in the race—and they were keeping pace with him. He turned and gave Molly a nod of respect for how well she was doing. She returned his nod, then he caught a sparkle in her eye as she shot ahead of him. Sorcha winked at him and Coll, who was a good ways back, before she burst ahead and followed Molly.

What in hellfire were they doing? If they kept charging ahead at that pace, they'd never be able to finish the race.

"Molly?" Tormod yelled, but she ignored him as she sped up. Not wanting to see her embarrassed, he called out to her again. "Molly, do not run yourself dry. You can finish."

She simply waved at him, then turned her head and grinned.

And hellfire if the lass did not speed up again. They were just about to cross into the fourth lap when he found himself tiring. How could Molly still be running that fast when he was running out of energy? Braden was still about even with him, but Coll had fallen far behind, along with the three Ramsay guards. Gavin and Gregor were ahead of him, but they could not catch Molly.

Gavin fell back when Molly had almost started her last circle. He moved next to Tormod and said, "You'll never catch her. 'Struth is, if this is the first time you've seen her run, 'tis best to stop and watch her. She's a sight to see. She deserves your full attention."

Tormod glanced from Molly to Gavin—and then back again. "She's done this before?"

Gregor laughed as he joined them. "All the time. She beats us all the time."

Tormod's chest felt as if it was about to burst, so he trotted to the side of the field and did just what Gavin had suggested. Molly suddenly sped up again as she crossed the line for the last lap. He'd never seen anything like it in his life.

Molly ran like the most graceful animal he'd ever seen. He was so flustered by her beauty he could not even think straight. Glancing around him, he found he was not the only one watching her. Everyone had stopped running, and Jamie was even applauding her. "Go, cousin!"

A deer. That's what she reminded him of, the fastest deer he'd ever seen. He'd never been great at hunting deer because their beauty stopped him every time. How could you not admire something that powerful, that strong, that surefooted as it did what it was meant to do?

Molly was a gifted runner.

"Amazing, is she not?" Jamie asked as he and Coll joined him.

Coll said, "A lass. How can a lass beat all of us?"

Jamie stood with his hands on his hips as Molly crossed the finish line and continued onward. Sorcha finished not far behind her, but was clearly no opposition for Molly. "Molly's always been the best runner. 'Tis her favorite thing to do, even more so than archery." He clasped Tormod's shoulder. "I cannot help myself. I love to fool lads into thinking they can beat her. She outran everyone at the first Ramsay festival. Uncle Logan couldn't stop cheering her on. Of course, when her mother trains anyone, running is part of it. 'Tis why Gavin and Gregor easily beat you and Coll. But I'm taking lessons from my aunt for our training."

"What do you mean?" Braden asked as he came up behind them.

"I'm guessing we do not have an easy battle ahead of us. 'Tis good to be prepared in as many ways as possible. So we shall train this way until Aunt Gwyneth and Uncle Logan return. I suspect it will happen within a sennight, and then we'll plan from there. Until then, we run." Jamie grabbed Braden's shoulder. "Grants included."

"And you, too?" Braden smirked.

"Aye. I'll join you on the morrow. This day was my chance to watch my cousin. Watch and learn."

The lads strode over to congratulate Molly on her win, but Tormod noticed something important.

Molly was surrounded by lads, but her gaze was on him.

CHAPTER SIX

MOLLY COULD NOT TEAR HER gaze from Tormod's. His eyes had locked on hers after she'd finished the race. His shock was evident. How she loved proving she was as good, or better, than a lad at anything.

Still a bit breathless, she accepted congratulations from those who waited to greet her at the finish line, but then waited patiently, hoping Tormod would come her way. Why this was important to her, she wasn't sure. She had no intention of courting anyone. Her goals were simple: become the best, make her parents proud, and then travel alongside her mother. Nowhere in that list was there anything about a lad. Getting married had never mattered to her, nor did having bairns sound enticing.

Nay, she'd prefer to stay the loner she was—and to take all the time she needed to practice archery and running and all the other skills that would make her useful to her parents. She wished to be free to make her own choices without waiting for another's opinion, and if she ever married, her freedom would end.

Now, if she could just understand her reaction to Tormod of the Grant warriors. As soon as he moved toward her, her heartbeat sped up, her palms began to dampen, and she felt as though she needed to clear her throat...over and over again. What the devil was happening to her? Prior to the race, she had found herself watching him closely, taking in the broad expanse of his chest and the way his muscles rippled when he held his bow, aiming for a target. Even his tongue had called to her.

He had this charming habit of sticking his tongue out between his lips when he concentrated, just a touch, but enough to tease her into wanting to press her lips to his and taste that tongue, something she'd never ever thought of doing before. True, she'd been kissed before because she was curious, but this was different. This was about what she wanted.

His light hair was in total disarray after running, sweat dotted his brow, and he had a smile on his face that she hoped was for her. He strode toward her, his gorgeous blue eyes dancing.

"Well done," Tormod said, still panting from exertion. "Have you always been able to run that fast, or has your training brought you to where you are today?"

Molly shrugged her shoulders, chewing on her lip. "My sire told me I was fast when he first saw me run, but he pushed me to run more. Mama and Papa have pushed us all to run, but they push me harder because I have the ability. At least, 'tis what my da says."

"They do not push Sorcha?"

"Aye, they do, but they think I can be the best. They love to see me enter contests. My mama gets excited when I run." She blushed and turned her face up to the sky. The clouds started to roll in at exactly the same moment the pain exploded in her head.

"Molly, what is it?" Tormod asked, rushing to her side.

She bent over at the waist and cursed. "My head aches again. I do not understand why. It just started."

Molly lifted her head again and stared up at the clouds rolling in quickly, some darker than others. A thunder cloud was headed their way.

Tormod said, "Come, let's see if we can get back before the storm hits." He put his arm around her to guide her, and together they ran toward the gates.

"Back inside the gates," Jamie shouted from behind them. "Sorcha, run as fast as you can. This storm is coming on us quickly, and 'tis most peculiar. Tormod, stay with Molly."

A few large raindrops fell from the sky, propelling them all toward the keep. They had made it inside the gates and were heading toward the stable when Aunt Avelina came running out of the keep. "Inside, Molly. Hurry," she shouted.

Molly stared up at the sky as she followed Aunt Avelina, unable to believe how much the sky had changed in such a short time. Her forehead scrunched as she saw two clouds moving in from opposite directions—a black storm cloud and a hanging cloud of darkness. When did that ever happen? Usually they all moved in the same direction. When the two clouds collided above them, the sky burst into a fury Molly had not seen before, drenching them in heavy rain and buffeting them with gusting winds. Tormod grabbed his plaid from his shoulder and placed it over her head, doing his best to shield her from the storm, but it raged with impossible fury.

Once inside, Tormod pulled his plaid from her head. The great hall, full of clan members escaping the rain, teemed with excitement and wonder at the strange storm. Molly listened to the chatter around her.

"I've never seen aught like it."

"A storm like that comes once in a lifetime."

"Did you see the dark clouds heading toward each other?"

"Aye, the two clouds appeared to be battling, did they not?"

Tormod ushered her over to the hearth and the roaring fire, and Aunt Avelina followed them. The temperature outside should have been cold enough to turn the rain to snow, yet it was rain that had fallen on them.

Someone else flew in the doorway, announcing to anyone who would listen, "Look, 'tis hailing now. Look how large the hail is!"

Molly sat near the hearth, rubbing her hands together. Tormod said, "I'll find you some warm broth, something to take the chill away." He headed toward the kitchen in search of a serving girl.

"Aunt Avelina, what did you think of the storm?" Molly asked. Her aunt sat in the chair next to her, pulled it close, and then reached over and straightened Molly's unruly curls. "It concerns me. It appeared to be two dark forces clashing. Did you notice aught unusual?"

Molly gave her a slow nod, almost hating to admit the truth. "Aye, my head pounded when the storm clouds started to roll in. The timing was unmistakable."

"Did you have a headache earlier today?"

"Nay. I had no ill effects from yesterday. I had just finished running a race, and you know how I love to run."

Aunt Avelina smiled and kissed her cheek. "Aye, I do. I'm glad you enjoyed it. You are stunning when you are in your glory."

Molly whispered, "Do you think it meant something?" She glanced over her shoulder, wanting to question her aunt before Tormod returned.

"Aye, I'm afraid I do."

"What?" She shivered as she waited for her aunt's response, somehow knowing what it would be.

"I had a dream last night. Someone bad has joined forces with MacNiven, and they are coming for us."

Ranulf MacNiven wiped the sweat from his brow with his plaid. How many days would this fever plague him? He glanced over at his second, Walrick, the only man who had stayed with him from the beginning. He'd lost many others. Fortunately, his most loyal companion survived.

Walrick wasn't the largest lad, but he was the cleverest one Ranulf had ever met. He knew how to stay one step ahead of the enemy. They'd met in the Highlands. Walrick was on the run for stealing from a clan, so he was as anxious for a new partner with coin as Ranulf was for a plan to escape the king's noose. They had struck a deal. Walrick would stay with MacNiven for one moon to earn his coin, and in that time, he would help him find a way to achieve his freedom. Permanently. There was only one small problem that he hoped to turn into an asset. Walrick had more ideas than Ranulf had ever thought of on his own. True, he'd thought of kidnapping someone to get what he wants. They'd done it in the past, the same as many clans. But Walrick was giving him bigger ideas, better ideas. He'd have to be watchful and careful, but the potential was there.

With Walrick's guidance, mayhap Ranulf MacNiven would be great again.

"How much longer will this fever last?" Ranulf spat a mouthful of green mucus off to the side of the crumbling hut. Without thinking, he rubbed the spot where the arrow had caught him. "Och! God's bones, it still pains me." He took another long swig of ale in the hopes it would help dull his pain.

"Be patient," Walrick said. "No one will find us here, which will give us plenty of time to plan. Now, have you agreed to my plan yet, or are you still entertaining the foolish idea of chasing back to the Grants for revenge on the one who shot you? We cannot fight them. They are too large. We'll have much better luck if we go to the Ramsays and enact my plan."

"I know 'tis what you think, but I'd still like to put my blade through whoever put this arrow in my shoulder." He wheezed as he set his head back down on the pallet. The arrow and the resulting fever had caused a serious delay in his plans. Walrick did not mind at all, but MacNiven hated being immobile.

"Aye, then ride to Grant land by yourself, try to track down the guilty party, and then find four hundred lads willing to fight for no coin, since you do not have enough to pay that many, and 'tis the number you'll need to have any hope of taking the Grants down."

"I understand. I've given up on the idea. Hellfire, I think you can see that I'm following your lead." MacNiven coughed and gagged on his own spittle.

"You must get to the south of England, as we discussed. 'Tis the only way you can escape the land of the Scots without a large boat. Once you're thinking clearly again, you'll realize I've given you a sound plan."

"What are the others doing?"

"Hunting, and the lasses are still sleeping."

Ranulf closed his eyes for a moment, reviewing his options. He just couldn't decide. Too many choices, and each gave him a special pleasure. "I remember. I must choose the person on whom I most wish to exact my revenge. Kidnapping that person will give us the leverage we need to get out of the country safely. And if the king does not give us what we want, then we can kill the Ramsay filth."

"So who shall it be?" Walrick sat in a chair, his arms crossed as he rested his boots up on the table.

Ranulf sighed, holding his head. "Tell me the choices again. My mind is weak."

"We could choose several from the Ramsay clan."

"But not the one I'd most wish to kill. The new laird."

"Aye, you'll never be able to get to the new laird. Like any chieftain, he surrounds himself with many men. We cannot risk facing them."

"Agreed. Who else?"

"I see four other possibilities. All are female, which makes them easier to control. You have the old laird's wife, the healer; or the new laird's wife; or one of the new laird's sisters."

"It cannot be the old laird's wife."

"Why not? You could use a healer about now."

"Because she's old. Besides, I would get little satisfaction from taking her. I hardly know her, and she's not caused any problems for me or the Buchans. Allow me a wee sense of satisfaction from this endeavor, please."

"And the other three have caused you problems?"

"Aye. Heather and Lily and Jennet have each caused their own problems. If it had not been for Heather, Torrian would have been more willing to marry Davina. That original plan was perfect. She's the one who caused all of our problems."

"Then Heather it is," Walrick said.

"Nay, not Heather. I want one of the sisters. 'Tis the best way to guarantee my freedom. The king will do aught for the old chief and his brother Logan, the spy. I want one of the chief's daughters, a niece of Logan Ramsay. I'll be granted my freedom for certes."

"Wise choice. I have a friend inside who already sent the fools a message in Edinburgh. I love to hear that they are frightened of us, especially when they don't know me. The smell of fear is all over Edinburgh, I'd wager. How I wish I was there to be witness to it." Walrick moved over to open the door and stared out over the land.

"I have a friend on Ramsay land who will do aught for the right amount of coin. I'll send him a message. By the time he gets it, we should be ready to move. All we need to do is find a safe place to hide during the negotiations. Probably the best place would be between Ramsay land and Edinburgh."

"We have a sound plan. Go ahead with it. Send your messenger, I'll be better by the morrow." Ranulf coughed and fell back on the pallet.

CHAPTER SEVEN

TORMOD ENTERED THE GREAT HALL for the evening meal the following day. He'd been chatting with Kyle, Torrian, Coll, and Jamie, but Torrian and Kyle left them as soon as they entered the cavernous space. The chieftain and his second made for the dais to join their wives, Heather and Lily, who was heavily pregnant, and Torrian's parents, Quade and Brenna.

Jamie patted Tormod on the shoulder. "Come this way. You're about to have a new experience. Join me at the cousins' table. We promise to entertain you."

"How many cousins do you have, Jamie?" Coll asked.

Jamie laughed. "Too many to count. I believe we number over thirty at last count. Though we are not all here, you'll be entertained by the ones who are."

They found spots at the trestle table, and Tormod glanced down the line at all who were seated. No sign of Molly. "Where are Molly and Sorcha?"

A young lass replied, "Maggie and Sorcha are both above stairs with Molly. She is suffering from a severe ache in her head. I've given her a potion to calm the pounding enough for her to sleep. I shall check on her soon."

Coll glanced at the lass, who appeared to be no more than seven summers. The wee lass was sitting beside another lassie, this one even younger. "*You* gave her a potion?" he finally asked.

"Aye, I am more than capable. I have been trained by the best healer in the land."

The lass next to her giggled. Their talk was interrupted when two serving girls brought over several trenchers along with a fresh loaf of bread for the table.

"Coll and Tormod, meet my cousin Jennet, Torrian's sister, and Molly's wee sister, Brigid. You already know Gavin and Gregor. I know, 'tis complicated, but just ask and I'll explain again." Jamie's gaze held a special gleam as he introduced his cousins.

Tormod stared at them all. "So Logan and Gwyneth have five children?"

"Aye," Brigid replied. "I am the youngest. Molly is the eldest, then Maggie, Sorcha, and Gavin."

"And Torrian, Lily, Bethia, Gregor, and Jennet belong to Uncle Quade and Aunt Brenna," Jamie explained.

"So you train with your mother, Lady Brenna?" Tormod asked Jennet, hoping to turn the conversation back around to Molly. "And did she check on Molly's progress?" He certainly hoped the clan's healer had not left the task to this wee lass.

Jennet had the most serious expression he'd ever seen on one so young. "Of course, she checked on my cousin. 'Tis her duty to tend to all the members of our clan, just as it is mine. She advised me that I'd chosen the correct treatment for Molly's problem." Jennet took a bite from the stew in her trencher.

Tormod stared at Coll, then at Jamie, not quite knowing how to respond to the lassie. While she was probably only about waist high, she spoke as if she'd lived five decades.

Brigid grinned and whispered to Tormod, "Do you see how smart my cousin is?"

Jennet replied without looking at her cousin. "Brigid, it has naught to do with intelligence. 'Tis all due to my superior training."

Coll choked on the piece of bread he'd been chewing. Gavin pounded him on his back, helping him to dislodge the food from his throat. "Jennet, you've confused another lad."

Jennet shrugged one shoulder and continued to eat her dinner. They'd each found a trencher and started to eat, chewing through the thick chunks of lamb and turnips, dipping their bread in the rich gravy.

Between bites, Gavin said, "We can tell you stories about Jennet and Brigid that will keep you laughing through the night."

"Aye," Gregor said. "I'm sure you've heard of the most famous one, how Jennet saved our brother Torrian from marrying Davina Buchan?"

Tormod set his bread down. "You? 'Twas you who showed that vial of blood to the king?" He turned to Jennet, who paid him little mind, continuing with her meal.

"Aye, though I've yet to comprehend the meaning of the entire fiasco. Why a simple vial of chicken blood could cause an entire court to erupt is beyond my understanding." Jennet continued to eat while Tormod and Coll stared at her with wide eyes and gaping mouths. "Much as I have tried to ask for a complete explanation from my sire, my mother will not allow it."

Brigid giggled, her hand over her mouth, and said, "Me, too. I do not understand."

A legend, he was conversing with a wee legend, and she had no idea how her actions had influenced the very fabric of the Highlands. Everyone in the land of the Scots had heard the tale of the wee lass who had outsmarted Ranulf MacNiven and the Buchans.

Glenn of Buchan had begged King Alexander to betroth his daughter, Davina, to Torrian Ramsay. Though Torrian had not wished to wed the lass, Davina's true love, Ranulf MacNiven, had played a cruel trick to make the king believe Torrian had taken the lass's maidenhead. He had been intent on using the marriage to gain power over the Ramsay clan. Since Davina had gone along with the ruse at the insistence of her father, the king had insisted on a betrothal. The Ramsays had protested, but the evidence—a set of bloody sheets from Torrian's chamber, presented after Davina had snuck inside—had seemed damning.

The two clans had been ready to battle in the middle of the royal castle in Edinburgh when wee Jennet had strolled over to Ranulf MacNiven and tried to give him a vial of chicken blood—one he'd requested while visiting Ramsay land. MacNiven had almost struck her, for she'd revealed his deception: he'd given Davina a vial of chicken blood to stain the sheets.

Jennet had saved the day for her brother. MacNiven had attacked the Ramsays against the king's order, after which he was convicted of treason and sentenced to hang. But the blackguard had paid someone to stand in his place.

The king's fury grew each day the man was still on the run. How Tormod hoped he would be able to take the villain down.

Gregor said, "You should hear about the other things my sister has done. She entertains us all year long."

"Aye, last year she made the biggest Ramsay guard pass out cold. He dropped to the floor like a lass, and it was completely Jennet's doing. She caused it with one of her experiments," Gavin said.

"Experiments?" Tormod chastised himself for sounding like a fool, but he couldn't seem to get more than one word out at a time.

Jennet said, "Again, I do not understand the fuss. I just wished to test my conjecture."

Every sentence that came from the lass shocked him more. "Conjecture? Where did you learn such a word? I'm not sure I know what it means."

Brigid giggled again. "Me neither. But Aunt Brenna says conjecture all the time."

Jamie cut in, "Understand that Jennet and Brigid spend most of their time with my Aunt Brenna." There was a fond smile on his face.

"Do you wish to hear about my experiment with the guard?" Jennet asked, turning to face Tormod.

Gregor and Gavin, who were out of her view, furiously nodded their heads, wide grins on both of their faces.

"Of course, do tell," Tormod drawled, leaning his cheek into his hand.

"You see, some people suffer from a strange affliction."

"Affliction?" Coll asked.

Jennet rolled her eyes. "Must I explain everything?"

"Nay, go ahead, lass." Jamie patted her shoulder.

"The affliction they suffer from is fainting whenever they see blood. My sire informed my mother that one of his guards suffered from such an affliction, and he did not know how he could allow this guard to go to battle because he would become useless on the battlefield."

"And what did your mother say?"

"My mother said she did not know if she could stop such an affliction, so I suggested the experiment. 'Twas truly quite simple." Jennet stopped in the middle of the story, her attention drawn to two guards who were walking past them. "Greetings, Bearchun."

The guard called Bearchun swung around and glared at Jennet, his finger pointed directly at her. "Do not talk to me, witchy girl. I do not trust you." Bearchun, a big burly beast of a man with beady eyes and a long beard, looked as though he could attack the wee girl easily. Not the usual caliber of guard that Tormod would expect to see on Ramsay land, but perhaps his sire had been part of the clan for years.

Tormod guessed Bearchun did not recognize Jamie, who was sitting close to where he was passing, else he would not have dared to speak to the old chieftain's daughter in that manner. Jamie's hand shot out and grabbed Bearchun by his plaid, yanking him close. "You'll speak to my cousin with respect or not at all."

Bearchun's gaze narrowed, but he spat out, "I'll choose not at all."

The big man's friend stood directly behind him. "I agree. We'll not speak to her. Bearchun, 'tis time to take our leave."

As soon as Jamie released the guard, he turned to face his friend. "Shaw, lead the way out of this hall. The stench makes me ill." They stalked away, and Bearchun glanced over his shoulder to glower at Jamie.

Tormod couldn't help but respect Jamie for standing up for his cousin. Jamie was not as large as Bearchun, but clearly he was much more muscular because he handled Bearchun with one hand.

Gavin said, "I'll have to take the time to tell Bearchun that you are Alex Grant's son. You'd think he would know better."

"How long has he been fighting for the Ramsays? He's of questionable character, if you ask my opinion." Jamie tapped his fingers sequentially against the table. "Someone needs to adjust his attitude."

"He came last summer," Gavin explained. "Said he knew Shaw's family. They are always together, Bearchun and Shaw. Most everyone stays far away from them. Shaw stokes the fire in Bearchun, loves to see him fight, but he is mighty on the battlefield with his fists." Gavin checked to make sure the lad had not returned. "I believe 'tis the one reason he's still here. He spends most of his time at Shaw's cottage."

"He's the one who dislikes Jennet," Brigid said. "Because of how she tried to test his 'fliction.'"

Tormod chuckled. "Do tell us more, Jennet."

"My mama told Papa that she did not think the sight of the blood would affect him if he was on the battlefield. Papa suggested we test it sometime, but Bearchun said nay, not in front of the others."

Gregor said, "And this is how my sister gets into trouble with Mama."

"Not your papa?" Coll asked.

"Nay," Gregor replied, "my da never scolds her. She's his wee bairn still."

"Nay, I am not a wee bairn, Gregor. Papa leaves the disciplining of the lassies to Mama." She gave her brother a haughty look before returning to her story. "Bearchun said nay to the test. My conjecture was that if we used red liquid that was not blood, 'twould not make him faint."

"So, how did you get in trouble with Bearchun?" Coll asked.

"And Mama?" Gregor added.

Jennet glowered at her brother, causing Brigid to giggle again. "I tested my conjecture on my own. I walked to the lists, pretended to cut myself, and poured the red liquid down my face in front of him. He fainted."

"And..." Gregor prompted.

"And all the guards were laughing at him when he awakened. Mama was upset with me, but I proved my conjecture wrong. I clearly demonstrated that it is the thought of blood that bothers him, not actual blood." The table erupted in guffaws. "Why are you laughing? 'Tis naught funny about his affliction."

"Aye, 'tis funny to me, lass," Jamie said.

"Me, too," Brigid said. She covered her mouth and turned away, giggling uncontrollably while all the lads laughed with her.

Jamie stopped his chuckle to say, "I see what you mean. You proved he would have trouble on a true battlefield. I'm sure he was not happy about that."

"Nay. I have other conjectures I would like to test, but Mama will not allow me near him."

Brigid sat up tall and announced, "She was not allowed in her mama's healing room for a sennight. 'Twas the worst punishment ever."

"Enough, Brigid." Jennet stared at her trencher. "No one understands me except Mama."

"I'm sure Aunt Jennie understands you," Jamie whispered as he leaned over to give her a squeeze. "You are special, Jennet. We love you even though we do not always understand you."

The door flew open with a bang, and Logan Ramsay came in with Gwyneth. He strutted straight toward them, his hand still entwined with his wife's. Jamie took one look at him and asked, "What is it?"

Brigid shouted, "Papa! Mama!" Gwyneth bent down and picked her up while Logan leaned over to kiss her cheek. Then he gave his full attention to Jamie, Tormod, and Coll. "Ashlyn put an arrow in MacNiven, and he's on the run again. We meet in my brother's solar."

◆———◦———◆

Molly had just come down the stairs when her parents came flying in through the front door. Her head felt much better so she'd decided to join the others in the hall, but she froze when she saw the look on her father's face.

She overheard his words to her cousin and his warriors. "Ashlyn put an arrow in MacNiven, and he's on the run again. We meet in my brother's solar." She stared at her mother as her father marched up to the dais, no doubt to speak with Uncle Quade and Torrian. Gwyneth spied her and stepped over to talk to her, Brigid still gathered in her arms.

Molly was afraid to ask the question she needed to ask. Finally, she managed to put her fear into words. "Is Ashlyn safe, Mama? Did she come with you?"

Her mother set Brigid down, gave her another kiss, and guided Molly into the solar. Molly's sire followed, along with his brother, Quade, and Torrian and Jamie.

"Sit, Molly. We'll explain all to you. Ashlyn is fine, but she chose to stay home."

Molly couldn't sit, so she remained standing, pacing a small corner of the solar. Torrian and Quade sat at their desks while the rest found seats. Molly's sire started, "First, Molly, your dream was true, and we thank you for it."

Her mother continued, "We found Ashlyn and Magnus deep in the Highlands. He was badly wounded and unconscious, and had we not come along, I believe he would have died. So we all owe you many thanks for that, daughter."

Molly fell into a chair, closing her eyes to say a quick prayer of thanks that Ashlyn and Magnus were both alive. Her dream had been correct, which meant she did have powers...powers that frightened her.

Her sire said, "Ashlyn and Magnus were caught in a snowstorm, and they stayed in an abandoned hut for two days before they could move on. When they did, they found tracks and followed them. MacNiven was in a crumbling keep. Magnus suffered a deep wound to his leg while fighting off several guards, but Ashlyn managed to put an arrow in MacNiven's shoulder before he left the property. Despite Magnus's wound, they made it within a day's journey of Grant land, which is where we found them."

Jamie turned to look at Molly, and everyone else followed his lead. "Molly, you have the gift of sight. You truly do."

She whispered, "But 'twas only a dream. Mayhap 'twill never happen again."

"But 'twas a true dream," her mother added, wrapping her arm around her shoulder.

"And how is Magnus?" Torrian asked.

"When we left, Magnus was recovering from the fever, though still weak. We wished to put Ashlyn in charge of the group of guards who came with us, but she declined. We suspect there will be a wedding between Magnus and Ashlyn."

"Truly?" Molly was shocked. Ashlyn had always been much like her, saying she had no interest in marriage.

"She's in love," her mother whispered to her, "and verra happy."

Molly still couldn't wrap her head around the sudden change, but she was happy for her cousin. "I hope Gracie is all right with that change."

"She will be. Ashlyn will stay on Grant land."

Molly's sire cleared his throat. "We need to move on. MacNiven is out there, and based on what Magnus overheard, he's heading south. He still has two women with him, but we know not where they go. Magnus thought his group numbered less than ten, but 'tis only a guess. We brought six more guards with us. We shall make our plans. I know we thought to stay here, but that was only when we had no knowledge of where MacNiven was. Now we know where he heads, so we shall send a team after him. Be prepared, we'll be leaving on the morrow or the next day, back toward Edinburgh or anywhere else the trail may take us."

Once the meeting ended, Molly moved into the great hall as if in a trance. She was a seer. While she'd hoped to be wrong about Ashlyn and Magnus, everything she'd seen in her dream had come to pass in some way. From this day forward, she would have to pay close attention to all her dreams.

Aunt Avelina led her over to a chair in front of the hearth. "I know exactly how you feel, lass."

"Do you, Aunt Lina?" She hoped her aunt could explain the power to her. She had so many questions.

"Aye. When I first found out I could see things, I became verra afraid of my powers. But there is no reason to fear what you can do and see."

"Do you have visions often?"

"Nay. Well, I dream every night, but they are not dreams about people I know, about predictions." Aunt Lina patted her hand.

"How will I know the difference?"

"You'll know. Predictions are different from normal dreams. They feel verra real, as if you are there with the person." Aunt Lina smiled at her. This new talent unfolding inside her was less frightening now that her aunt was around. She had the same ability, after all, and it had not made her life unhappy. "Tell me about some of your other dreams."

"In one of them, I saw a man throw a lass over a horse and ride away with her, but I could not see who it was."

"And did it come true?"

Her shoulders slumped. "Aye. I had the dream after Mama, Sorcha, and I arrived in Edinburgh. I told my sire as soon as we saw him, so he turned around and rode right back to Jamie's team."

"Why did he do that?"

"Because I dreamed of a lass, and Ashlyn was traveling with the Grant team. They'd been attacked and she'd been tossed over a horse, just like in my vision, but Magnus saved her."

"How about before that? Have you had any you did not understand?"

Molly thought for a while, recalling some unusual dreams that had upset her an uncommon amount. There had been plenty of those, only most of them had been so shadowy and unclear there was naught to say about them. "Only one other. I dreamed a lass had been stolen from Edinburgh."

"When was that?"

Molly gasped aloud. "It happened around the time Lily had been kidnapped. The dream was so unclear, I did not recognize it for what it was. Now I'm wondering if it was Lily in my dream. Mayhap I could have helped." She wrung her hands together.

"Nay, do not feel guilty," Aunt Lina said, taking her hands. "My first dreams were the same. There was never enough information for me to recognize them for what they were. But they became stronger, more detailed. The more I had, the more I could remember. You'll see. Promise me you'll not fear them. They will never hurt you. But whenever you have a vision, you must inform your da or Uncle Quade or me."

"Can I try to have a vision Aunt Lina? If I need information?"

"Nay, I wish it were that easy, lass. You never know when a dream will come. And I can tell you that sometimes they come when you least expect them."

CHAPTER EIGHT

MOLLY COULDN'T SLEEP. THE FEAR of another dream full of dire predictions prevented her from being able to relax. She stepped out of the chamber she shared with Maggie and Sorcha and headed toward the end of the passageway to go up to the parapets. Her sire used to take her there after her parents first brought her and Maggie to Clan Ramsay.

She opened the door and tugged the plaid more tightly around her when she felt the cold wind blast her face. She did not mind the cold at all—it kept her awake and alert. Her mind traveled back to one special day with her adoptive sire.

Her true sire had convinced Molly that she was worthless. Logan Ramsay had done everything in his power to convince her she did have value, and moreover, that her true sire had been a fool.

Hog droppings.

Those had been Logan's exact words every time she'd confided one of her true sire's beliefs to him. She smiled at the beloved memory of the conversation they'd had up here on the parapets one day.

"Papa says I'm a terrible cook."

"Hog droppings," Logan had said. "Did he try to show you how to cook? Cooking is learned. If he could not teach you, then 'tis his fault, not yours."

"When I tried to make soup, he called me boil-brained." The sad truth was that she recalled nearly every insult her father had ever thrown at her—and they still had the power to make her cry.

"Hog droppings, I say," Logan repeated with conviction. "Your sire is an arse."

She covered her mouth upon hearing Logan Ramsay cuss in front of her, especially about her father. Then she recalled another insult. "Once, when my mama tried to make us all pretty, he said everyone looked fine except for me." She swallowed the lump in her throat to force herself to continue. With the barest of whispers, she confessed to her biggest embarrassment. "He called me goatish. And everyone laughed, and I was called a goat every day after that by my brothers."

Logan was quiet for a long moment, but his knuckles went white where he gripped the side of the parapet. Finally, he turned toward her and lifted her chin until her gaze met his. "You will always be beautiful to me, lass, because 'tis what's inside that counts most, and you have the biggest heart I've seen in a long time. You put others' needs in front of your own. And I also think you are quite pretty. You have doe eyes, the eyes of the most graceful creature on the earth."

It was a comment she'd tucked away in her mind and savored many times over the years. She peered up at him then and asked him a most difficult question. "May I call you Papa? I'd like to forget my true papa." One tear found its way down her cheek, and Logan Ramsay swiped it away.

"Naught would please me more. Your true sire is an old goat for not recognizing your worth. And a surly pig-nut, a term my friend Loki likes to use. It fits your sire...goatish, surly pig-nut that he is. I'd like to see him and tell him what he's lost. But pay him no mind. You'll be our daughter from now on, you and Maggie are Ramsays."

That had been one of the happiest days of Molly Ramsay's life. It was the first day she'd ever truly felt loved by anyone other than Maggie. Now it was her turn to make Logan Ramsay proud. She would do all she could to help them catch MacNiven, and if she were lucky, word of her family's accomplishments would pass back to her true sire.

A voice interrupted her thoughts as she leaned over the cold stone. She jerked up and looked back, only to see Tormod behind her. There was a wide smile on his face as he said, "Molly? Why are you here? 'Tis mighty cold, is it not?" He pulled the plaid, which had slipped while she was lost in thought, back up over her shoulders.

"Aye, but it does not bother me. I love the outdoors."

"You'd be the first lass I've heard admit that. Why are you not sleeping?"

She twisted away from him to lean on the stone of the wall again, and he took the spot next to her. Just like earlier, on the archery field, she was struck by Tormod's handsomeness. Even in the dark of night, she could make out his pale brown hair, which, she'd noticed earlier, had strips of gold here and there, as if the sun had painted some of the strands. His eyes were blue, but they also had a touch of gold to them. The dusting of stubble on his chiseled jaw made her wish to reach out and touch him. He was tall and broad-shouldered, just the right amount of muscle. Not huge like Magnus, but more lean and probably more agile. Is this what had happened to Ashlyn? Had she changed her mind about being alone because she'd met the man who made her heart beat faster?

"Something wrong?" he asked, his gaze narrowing on her as he took a step closer, leaning in toward her.

She could feel the blush cross her face. "Nay. I just cannot sleep. I used to come up here with my sire."

"Someday you'll have to tell me all about how it feels to be Logan Ramsay's daughter. It must have been difficult at times. Was he hard on you? Is that why you excel at all you do?"

She giggled. "Nay. The only thing my adoptive sire has done is love me. Just being accepted as his daughter is enough motivation for me to push myself."

"And your true sire did not love you?"

"Nay, he gave me and my sister away." She stared up at the stars, not wanting him to see how much this still hurt her despite how the years had dulled the pain. Her parents had helped her realize that she was talented and had much to offer.

"Molly?" Tormod leaned closer toward her.

She had no idea what he was about to ask her, but he was awfully close, close enough for her belly to start doing wee flips, and for her heart to speed up. She could feel the dampness in her palms even though she was outside in the middle of a cold night. Why did she react so to him? "Aye?"

"Have you ever been kissed?"

She nodded, unable to think of anything to say. Aye, she'd been kissed, but it had been awkward curiosity and nothing more, playful youth that she and Sorcha had planned. While she'd had some experience, it was very different than this, the way her heart raced whenever Tormod was near, the way the heat of his gaze melted her thoughts into oblivion.

She jumped when his lips descended on hers, the warmth melting her insides enough for her to part her lips. His tongue swept between her lips as he moved closer, closing the gap between them enough for him to enfold her inside the heat of his embrace. She was lost in his arms, wondering if she should do the same with her tongue, venturing timidly to touch his. He groaned, clutching her closer, tighter against his body so she could feel the hardness of his upper arms. His chest felt like a rock, and she had no idea how to react when he continued his assault on her lips, other than to mimic him.

Except that everything about Tormod felt wonderful. This was not at all what she'd expected.

She jerked back suddenly at the sound of the door creaking open, and Tormod stepped away from her. Jamie's eyes widened as soon as he stepped through the doorway and saw them.

Molly took one look at Jamie and ran down the staircase and down the passageway, but she had nowhere to run.

What had just happened?

Jamie raised a brow at Tormod. "Never forget who her sire is, lad. I trust you'll use good judgment."

Tormod nodded. "Excellent advice, and I shall take it. I know not what possessed me just now." He rubbed his chin as if it could bring back the luscious lips he'd been tasting.

Damn, but he hadn't expected Molly to taste that good, or to fuel his desire as much as she had. Though he was unable to recall what had prompted him to kiss her, mayhap it had been a good move. Now that he'd accomplished his goal, he was certain he would be able to stop thinking about the beautiful lass.

Only that plan was already not working. He scratched his head, wondering what had gone wrong.

"Tormod?" Jamie asked, leaning toward him.

"Aye, Jamie? Do you need my help with something?" He had to force Molly out of his mind and focus on the man in front of him.

"I'm not going to ask what you were doing with Molly, but I hope you did not bring her up here yourself. You know how that could be misconstrued. You were alone with the lass."

"Nay, I mean, I know of what you speak, but nay. She was already here when I came up."

Jamie arched his brow at him.

"What kind of fool do you take me for? God's teeth, nay."

"See that you keep it that way. I do not care to see my uncle on a rampage, and trust me, he would be if he thought any of his daughters had been wronged." Jamie shifted his attention from Tormod to the view over the stone parapet. "Never did understand why my sire loved to be up in the parapets back home. He goes out there most every night except when the winds are in a fury or if my mother needs him."

Tormod leaned on the stones next to Jamie and stared out over the land. "Mayhap when 'tis your own, you'll understand."

"I do not think Grant land will ever belong to me, but mayhap it would feel different if it were mine."

"The land will belong to both you and Jake."

"Jake was born first. 'Tis the way of our ancestors, and Jake will be a strong laird. I accept that."

"I see your sire handling the lairdship differently. A strong-minded leader like him will do as he sees fit, not as others see as fit." Tormod actually felt more of a kinship with Jamie than he did with Jake, though he liked and respected both brothers. Jake was much more intense, like his sire, while Jamie knew how to relax and enjoy himself. Jamie laughed more. While both were strong swordsmen, since their sire would not have it any other way, they had different fighting styles, too. Jake was more likely to take charge and attack full-force while Jamie stayed back and observed, finding the enemies' weaknesses before he acted.

Jamie moved over to the door and tugged it open, "If you do not mind, I'd like to head downstairs for an ale. Join me?"

Tormod followed him. "Aye. 'Tis a wee bit cold up here." The great hall was mostly empty when they arrived, other than a few servants cleaning the trestle tables. Quade and Logan Ramsay sat near the hearth, both of them staring into the fire.

Logan was the first to notice their arrival. "Sit, lads. Tell me what's been on your minds of late. Any new theory on where we should go first or how we should handle this situation?"

Quade smiled at the two of them. "Aye, I'd like to hear what the other young minds are thinking. Torrian just left for his chamber."

Jamie said, "We have not discussed it, but I think we need to leave as soon as possible. We mustn't give MacNiven the chance to move too far ahead of us."

"Aye, I cannot disagree with you," Logan said, staring at his ale, his elbows leaning against his knees. "Mayhap we'll leave when the sun is the highest."

A few minutes later, the sound of a scream carried into the hall from a chamber above stairs—the kind of scream that would chill the queen of the ice castles. All four of them bounded out of their chairs and headed toward the sound, only to be stopped in a second.

Molly leaned over the balcony railing, screaming, "Jennet, something has happened to Jennet and Brigid." Logan raced up the stairs with Jamie directly behind him. Quade's knee preventing him from moving quickly, so Tormod stayed below with him—ready to race outside if need be. Sorcha and Maggie came out of the bed chamber Molly had just left, rubbing their eyes.

Logan headed straight for the lassies' bed chamber, but Molly stopped him. "Nay. They're not there."

Quade yelled up at the others from below stairs. "What is it? What happened to the lassies? Where are they?"

Brenna came flying down the passageway, almost running into Logan where he stood on the balcony overlooking the hall. "Molly, where's Jennet? I heard you say her name."

"I do not know. I fell asleep with Maggie and Sorcha, and I had a terrible dream that something had happened to Jennet and Brigid. Something's wrong. I'm sure of it." She clutched her head in the next moment and moaned, falling to the floor. Logan barely managed to catch her before her head hit the floor.

Tormod flew up the stairs, no longer willing to wait. He crouched by Molly's side to see if she was hale. "Molly? Can you speak to us, lass?" Her breaths came out in pants, her teeth clenched in a fight against the pain.

"My head. 'Tis the worst ever. It must be someone terrible, something awful."

Tormod moved his arm underneath her neck to support her, not caring what her sire thought. She curled into him and gripped his forearm, still gasping in pain. Her sire stood, apparently willing to accept Tormod's assistance, so he continued nursing her. "Take a deep breath, lass."

Molly whispered, "I'll be all right. Find them, please."

"Brenna, check their chamber," Logan barked.

She did his bidding, but screamed when she opened the door to the lassies' room.

Quade bellowed. "What is it? Where are they?" He moved to the stairway and tugged himself up each step, clearly in pain judging by the movement of his knee.

Tormod helped Molly to sit, then followed Jamie into the chamber behind Brenna, coming up behind her as she rushed over to the bed. Her daughter, Bethia, was tied up on the bed, and tears were streaming down her face as she struggled with her bonds.

Brenna tried to undo the ropes with shaking hands, but Jamie stepped in, cutting the bindings on the lass's hands while Tormod freed her legs. Brenna removed the gag in her mouth.

"Jennet, they took Jennet and Brigid."

Logan appeared in the doorway. "Who took them?"

Bethia coughed, clearing something from her mouth. "Bearchun. He was the only one I recognized. There was another with him, but I did not know him. They gave them something that made them sleep, then put each one in a sack and carried them out the door. I heard them move in the direction of the back staircase to the kitchens."

"Did anyone see them?" Logan looked around at everyone while Brenna sat on the bed, hugging Bethia.

Jamie said, "Nay, Tormod and I were in the parapets. And we were looking at the mountains rather than the courtyard. But Bearchun could walk right through the gates. He would not be stopped. He's a Ramsay warrior."

Quade finally appeared in the doorway, his stance pained. "Find him, Logan," he snarled. In his next breath, he hollered for his sons, "Torrian, Gregor!"

"Lads, come with me," Logan said, turning to Tormod and Jamie, who followed him down the passageway. Logan stopped to kiss Molly along the way, "Thank you, lass. You've done it again. Sorcha, go awaken your mother."

Tormod took one look at Molly and fought the need to gather her up in his arms like he had at Castle Edinburgh. He could see how much her head was paining her, but he could not make such a declaration in front of her father. Not when he needed to go after Bearchun.

Jamie whispered, "The war has begun."

CHAPTER NINE

MOLLY HELD HER HEAD AS the pain began to subside. Her mother came flying down the passageway, followed by Aunt Avelina and Uncle Drew. Her uncle flew down the stairs along with a few unidentified others that must have come from the other direction to join the chase, but her mother and aunt helped her up and led her into Bethia's chamber. Her sisters trailed in behind them.

After Brenna explained what had happened, her eyes filled with tears, Aunt Avelina turned back to Molly. "Lass, please sit and think hard. Tell us all you remember from your dream. There could be something important you forgot to tell us."

Molly sat on the bed between her mother and Aunt Avelina. Aunt Brenna was holding Bethia, but her gaze was fixed on Molly. Sorcha and Maggie were sitting on the floor in a heap, both of them weeping.

Molly rubbed her temple and closed her eyes. "I'm trying to recall, but it was so dark. I saw two men carrying Jennet and Brigid in a cart, but then they joined a group of men. And they all ran. They ran and ran and ran…I'm sorry. 'Tis all I remember."

"Did you hear aught? Were there any names mentioned?"

"The only thing I heard was Jennet consoling Brigid. She told her they were smarter than the men, and they'd get away."

Gwyneth smiled. "That sounds just like your daughter, Brenna. They are strong together. They'll stay sharp, I believe. We must go after them."

Aunt Brenna said, "The men have already left. It will not help us if you leave separately."

"Nay," said Gwyneth. "But I know my husband's methods. They'll return if they do not find any leads, and we'll split into teams. Molly and Sorcha, get dressed. We'll need archers on both teams. Molly will be going with me, Sorcha with her sire. Brenna, you and Avelina will stay to see if any messages come to you."

Aunt Avelina rubbed Molly's shoulder. "Will you be able to be ready? Maggie can run down and find you something to eat. 'Twill help you. I'll find Aunt Brenna's potions, give you something to help ease the ache in your head. It may continue until they are found. And do not be afraid to sleep."

"We will not have time to sleep until we find them," Gwyneth said.

Aunt Avelina replied, "You may have to if you cannot find them. Molly could have another dream giving you a clue to their location. 'Twill only happen if she sleeps."

Molly did not wish to think of it, but she knew that her dear sister and cousin were missing, and she would do aught to find them. She stood up and grabbed Sorcha's arm. "Come, we'll get ready."

An hour later, Torrian, Uncle Logan, Tormod, Coll, Gavin, Gregor, and Kyle came bounding into the great hall, dire expressions on their faces.

They moved to the hearth, and Brenna sent the serving lasses for ale and meat pies. Her gaze hopeful, Molly glanced at her father, but the expression on the men's faces did not bode well for the two lassies. Sorcha, who sat next to her, squeezed her hand.

Logan dropped into a chair, wiping the sweat from his brow, and Torrian took the seat next to him. "We followed their tracks to the creek, but we could not pick them up again."

"How many?" her mother asked. Molly's mind had turned to mush, but her mother's and father's minds clicked together with amazing speed and efficiency.

"Initially, there were two horses. And Shaw is also missing. So we'll refer to them as Bearchun and Shaw. The two caught up with another three horses on the far side of the long meadow. They traveled for a while, but then turned toward the river. They crossed, as did we, though the waters are getting deep and cold for the horses. Alas, we never picked up their trail on the other side. I've thought this through." The serving lasses arrived with tankards of ale and meat pies. Logan nodded to the men. "Eat while you have the chance. We'll be leaving soon."

He took a few mouthfuls of food before continuing. "No need to wolf your food down, lad," he said to Coll. "We are not leaving for a couple of hours yet."

"Logan, we cannot wait that long."

"Aye, we can, Gwynie. We need daylight to pick up their trail again. We'll be running blindly in the dark. I know you wish to follow them now, but 'twould be fruitless. We'll leave just before daybreak. We shall split into teams. Gwynie, you are to take Molly, Tormod, and four guards with you. I've already given my instructions to the guards who are to travel with you. You need to move quickly, see if you can catch them. They were wise to use the river to throw us off, but I'm quite sure with the small amount of snow, they'll be traveling where the sun is warm enough to melt it and erase their movements. I know which trail they are taking."

He stopped to take another bite of food. "My team will take the shorter path to Edinburgh, hoping to slip ahead of them. With the lassies, their travel could be slowed, and I do not think they will risk exposing themselves on the well-traveled road. This way we can close in on them.

"I'm sure they are headed toward Edinburgh, just as I'm sure they only took the lassies to use them as bargaining chips. We anticipated this...we just didn't expect two of our own to turn against us. I do not think they will venture into the actual village, so we should focus our efforts in the area about a half day's ride from the royal burgh, mayhap a day's ride. They'll need to be close to negotiate with the king. My team will go directly to the area I suspect, and hopefully we shall arrive before they do."

"Are you sure they will not take the direct route?" Quade asked. "Explain your reasoning again, please."

"They're traveling with young lassies who could slow them. My guess is they've planned out a couple of stops on the way to the burgh. There are only a few places to hide off the fastest route, so we would catch them easily there. Nay, they'll take the longest way in the hopes of losing us. If they hide themselves well, we could fly directly past them on the main route without realizing it. You know this land."

Quade nodded, his brow furrowed. "Please explain your choices for the teams?"

"Easiest question to answer. Gwynie and Molly both move faster that I can, are better at hiding in the trees, and can stop the enemy from a greater distance. There are at least five with Bearchun, plus the two girls. My wife and daughter can take four of them out before the target even realizes they've been hit. Tormod's skills with the arrow are improving, too. I take Sorcha and Gavin for my shooters. Gregor…I'll leave as your choice."

At first Molly didn't understand what her father was asking her uncle, but then she recalled the unspoken rule of warriors. All of one family never traveled together. He was giving Uncle Quade and Brenna the choice of sending Gregor or keeping him here with them, since two of their children, Torrian and Jennet, were already at risk. She saw Uncle Quade turn his gaze to Aunt Brenna, obviously leaving the decision for her.

Aunt Brenna whispered, "Send him. We must put a stop to this. Send him with Gwyneth. The women have better instincts, and Jennet and Brigid will be a handful for the men. I'll have Maggie, Bethia, Heather, Nellie, and Lily here with me."

The decision was made, so they all found places to sit and strategize. Tormod moved over to join his team, sitting next to Molly. He leaned in and whispered, "How is your head? Still paining you?"

There was much discussion and planning taking place in the hall, and it felt as if it were the middle of the day in the cavernous room. There was so much going on that Molly was comfortable talking to Tormod without being overheard. "I took a potion to dull the pain. 'Tis tolerable now."

"How does it feel to bear so much responsibility? Imagine if you had not had that dream? Bethia may not have been discovered until morning."

"Bethia usually sleeps late. I'm thankful I had the dream, but I know not what will come to pass." She stared at her hands in her lap and whispered to him, "It frightens me."

Tormod reached over to take her hand in his. "It would scare the hell out of me."

Molly didn't understand why or how, but just the touch of his hand heated her entire body, and she found it quite appealing.

◆———○———◆

Ranulf MacNiven wanted to shout for joy as soon as his gaze settled on four of his men coming toward him, two of them with sacks lying across their horses' backs, sacks just the right size to be carrying bairns. He moved into the cave and spoke to the women sleeping on the floor. "Get up, both of you. You've work to do."

Cedrica sat up and stared at him. "What work? I thought I was your lass? Make Lorna do it."

"I need you both. There are two lassies for you to watch. I'll give one to you and one to Lorna."

Cedrica reached out and tugged on Lorna's arm. "Lorna, we must get up. Come. Move."

Lorna yelled, "Cedrica, I'm getting up. Leave me be."

Ranulf leaned over and grabbed both of her cheeks in one hand. "I said to get up. You have work to do. I protect you and feed you, so you have certain expectations to satisfy."

"But I thought you were just taking us to the place of women in Edinburgh. We were going to make plenty of coin. We promise to share. I do not wish to do aught else in the forest. Critters frighten me." She did her best to get away from him, but to no avail.

"Nay, you have work to do before we arrive in Edinburgh. Now get ready. How hard can it be to handle a lass of six or seven summers?"

He didn't drop his hand until she sat up. "That's my good lass." He wouldn't allow the two bitches to ruin this for him. This had been the main reason he'd brought them along, to take care of anyone he stole along the way. Once he got to Edinburgh, he planned to sell the two of them to a man who'd promised to pay a huge amount of coin for lasses who would spread their legs, though he hadn't explained it to them in quite the same way.

He moved back out of the cave, a grin on his face as he watched Bearchun struggle with the wee lass in his arms.

It would seem the two of them had been unable to steal his first choice, Lily, but no matter. He'd been successful. As soon as they were close enough, he yelled the most important question. "They're still alive?"

"Aye, this one's been crying and wiggling," Bearchun said, "enough to make me want to throw her off the horse, but the one he's carrying hasn't moved at all."

"Hand her to me, I wish to see if she's still alive. I'll decide what to do with them."

Bearchun's companion handed the sack to MacNiven, and Ranulf set her down on the grass, kneeling next to her and untying the end before he pulled on the wee legs sticking out. They were still warm—a promising sign of life. He couldn't stop the grin on his face. Finally, he held a true bargaining chip to use against the great Ramsay clan, the clan who'd put an end to his reign as laird, crushed all his hopes and dreams, and almost put him in the hangman's noose.

Now he was in control. The bastards would pay. Soon the Ramsays and the king would be giving in to all of his demands.

Every single one. He'd have to take his time to carefully consider the demands he'd like to make. This scheme of his had been perilous at times, but he'd made it. He'd have them on their knees begging him, willing to give him everything he wanted.

He tugged on the feet to pull the lass out of the sack. As soon as her head cleared the bag, she pushed her arms down and sat up with a vengeance, bringing her face within inches of his.

It was Jennet, the one who'd started all his problems, the one who'd pursued him with the inauspicious vial that had changed everything.

For some odd reason, he did not move, staring into her eyes, seeing if she would challenge him. He waited, because if she dared to cause him any problems, he would thrash her bottom, tie her up, shove a gag into her mouth, hang her upside down from a tree, tease her with a snake—any number of tortures came to mind in an instant.

"You're enjoying this, are you not?" Bearchun said with a chuckle.

MacNiven moved his face closer to the lassie's, expecting her to back away, waiting for her to recognize him and back away in fear. In his most chilling tone, he asked, "Remember me?"

But she didn't move. Instead she moved a wee bit closer, their noses almost touching. Her gaze narrowed, and she whispered, "Do you remember me? Because I'm a witch."

Her voice was barely audible except the last word "witch" came out in a screech that sent him bolting up from the ground. The wee bitch had said the one word that had a way of digging deep into his mind, sending tendrils of eerie possibilities curling into the furthest corners of his brain.

A witch. Naught frightened him more.

"You must watch her," Bearchun barked. "She is a wee spiteful witch." He set his sack down on the ground, holding it tight as it tossed one way and then the other. "Stop it, you miserable bitch." He raised his hand to swat the end of the sack, but MacNiven caught it mid-air.

"You'll not be touching them. They are mine to do with as I choose."

"As you wish," Bearchun replied, "but get her to end the screaming and crying, will you not?" He stood up and stalked off toward the trees.

MacNiven opened the sack, then rolled the lass out of the bag. "Well, well, who are you, lassie?"

The lass let out a screaming howl that grated up his spine. "Cease, will you not?" She did not see reason.

Bearchun returned, his hands still putting his trews back in place. "Convince her to stop or give me the pleasure of snapping her wee neck. 'Twill snap like a twig."

Jennet said, "Do that, and I'll curse you. I'll make blood drip from your ears and your nose." Then she stared straight at Bearchun. "You know I can do it. Leave her with me and she'll settle."

MacNiven couldn't believe the response she received from Bearchun.

The man actually hid behind a tree. "You stay away from me, you wee witch."

"What is it?" he asked in bafflement.

The other lass still had her head tipped back in an ear-piercing scream. What the hell. He tugged on both ends of his long hair, trying to awaken his reason. He had two Ramsays, or so he guessed. He glanced at Bearchun, still hiding behind that tree as if a giant bear stood in front of him instead of a lass under eight summers. He pointed to the screaming twit. "Is she a Ramsay?"

"Aye, she's Logan Ramsay's daughter. Give the witch what she wants for now. Get her to stop staring at me."

MacNiven tipped his head back, a rumbling laugh bursting out from him. Hellfire, but it could not be more perfect. Perhaps he'd keep Bearchun alive for getting him one of each. The sister of Torrian Ramsay and the daughter of Logan and Gwyneth, the famous spies. He'd have to keep them both. He grabbed the screaming girl by the arms and held her up over Jennet. "If you promise to keep her quiet—and not to curse us—I'll let her be with you."

Jennet nodded, holding up her arms in time to catch the lass as he dropped her. The girl threw her arms around Jennet, her screams ebbing as Jennet consoled her.

"What's her name?"

Jennet glared at him, her lips pursed.

"Tell me or I'll throttle you both. I'll keep you together, but tell me her name."

Bearchun said, "It starts with a B, but I cannot recall."

Jennet locked her gaze on him as she wrapped her arms around her cousin. "Brigid. Her name is Brigid. Now leave us be."

Brigid rested her head on Jennet's shoulder, her breath hitching from all the screaming and crying, but at least the infernal screeching had stopped.

Ranulf snickered, clasping his hands together in front of him. "Perfect. I could not be in a better position."

"What's next?" Bearchun asked.

"We have to pee!" Jennet shouted.

"Cedrica, move your arse. I need you out here."

A distant shriek came out of the nearby cave. "We'll be there soon. You did not give me much time."

MacNiven turned to her, waving at the trees next to them. "Go in the trees, but know if you take off, I'll thrash Brigid so hard, she won't be able to cry again."

Jennet lifted her chin, took Brigid by the hand, and stalked off into the woods. She was a feisty lass, he had to give her that. Too bad she wasn't a bit older.

Ranulf said, "We move toward Edinburgh. I have chosen the perfect place for us to hide while I send my message off to the king. The Ramsays will never find us there."

He paced the clearing, then realized the lassies should have returned by now. He ran over to the area, and let out a breath when he found them—Brigid standing and fiddling with her clothes, and Jennet sitting by the tree, hitting it with a stick.

"Enough. We're leaving."

He tossed them each on a horse before climbing up behind Jennet. He'd have to keep an eye on this one, for sure.

The Ramsays would find out very soon that *he* was in control this time.

CHAPTER TEN

TORMOD HAD TO ADMIT HIS gut clenched through the whole morn. They'd set out at first light, anxious to find the tracks Logan could not find in the dark. Molly's mother led next to her, but each of them were flanked by a Ramsay guard. Tormod and Gregor rode behind them, with two other guards bringing up the rear. They easily tracked the attackers to the river, then Molly and her mother dismounted their horses to search more closely for anything that could give them a clue as to what direction the kidnappers had traveled. A few minutes after they'd started to look, Gwyneth said, "Here. I can tell a few horses moved through here."

Tormod and the guards remained on horseback to protect the women, but he watched with great interest as Molly hurried to her mother's side. Gwyneth pointed to the broken branches. "They moved through the densest part of the forest, hoping we wouldn't venture into it. But we know this area, so they could not have followed inside the trees for long. There is only one place they could have exited. She pointed to their horses. "Follow me."

Molly and her mother led the way through the thicket, ignoring the heavy frost that had covered the bare branches of the trees with a hard silvery coating. At the earliest in the day, the trees had appeared quite eerie to Tormod, though the others seemed quite use to the crackling of the branches as they moved in and out of the woods.

Almost an hour later, they came to a spot that had clearly been trampled by horses, and the rest of the kidnappers' tracks were easy to find.

Molly and Gwyneth led them through a large glen, and they continued to follow them with no problem. Tormod had to admit that the beauty of the landscape took his breath away. From the craggy knolls to the moorland slopes, the outdoors was beautiful, but this was not the time to slow and appreciate it.

It was not until midday that they seemed to have lost their path.

Gwyneth dismounted, pacing in a circle as she searched the area for any clues. Molly joined her, but they found nothing.

Gwyneth guided them into the center of the small clearing. "Gregor, you go with me through this area." She pointed south of their location after they'd all dismounted. "Tormod, you and Molly go check in that direction. Meet back here in half of the hour. We must find the correct path as quickly as possible. I'll leave the guards in the periphery."

Molly nodded, checked the sun, and then glanced back at Tormod. "Come, we have no time to lose."

Shite, but the lass was quick. He followed her into the brush, up and down the slopes of the Highlands, slipping here and there due to the dampness from the morning frost that was now melting. It was no easy task, but somehow, he managed to keep up with her. This was not a practice run, and he vowed to do everything he could to save those girls. He'd been searching all his life for a way to prove that he was worthy, and this was it. True, he did not have the training that Molly did when it came to tracking, but if he stayed with Molly, he might get a chance to face Ranulf MacNiven, the scoundrel who'd had the gall to kidnap the Ramsay brothers' daughters. Catching MacNiven could put his name in the minstrels' tunes for all to hear. His name would even be known to their king...their king!

He'd never have a better chance to make his sire proud. Another pull called to him, to his surprise. He wished to help Molly. Her ability to focus, her drive to be the best, motivated him almost as much as his own purpose.

"Molly, tell me what to look for. I have not had much training in tracking, but I'd like to learn." He raced behind her, his breath already coming out in pants because of the speed she kept, but he truly wished to be of assistance to her.

Molly glanced over her shoulder. "I'll slow as I check this area and explain as I go."

"Great," he huffed out, unable to believe how far they'd just traveled. "You move so fast, it's a wonder you don't miss things."

She ignored him but began her instruction. "You need to look for tracks in the ground. The ridges from hoof prints are more visible when then sun reflects across the ground, especially after a frost. You should also search for any broken branches, scraps of food that might have been tossed down from a mount, leaves in an unnatural pile designed to hide something, or even horse droppings. You may see a piece of wool caught on a branch or even hair fibers if someone is running."

Her gaze scanned the area, but she looked almost frantic—too wound up to truly focus. "Molly? I know she's your sister, but has your mother not taught you how to stay calm?"

She glared at him before returning her gaze to their surroundings. "I cannot stay calm. This is my test. I must do well. If I can help find MacNiven, my name will be known and…"

"And what?"

She didn't answer, instead shaking her head and moving through the trees.

"I have thought the same." His voice echoed behind her.

She halted in her tracks and spun around to scowl at him. "What are you talking about?"

"Finding MacNiven. I wish to help find him to clear my name."

Her hands rested on her hips. "What is wrong with your name? I've heard naught."

"'Tis nothing you would have heard about. They're family issues."

"Such as?"

She didn't move as he'd hoped. It was hard for him to think clearly when her huge brown eyes settled on him, long lashes framing her gaze. Her curly hair was plaited, yet she was still stunning, her skin so smooth that he longed to brush his fingertips across her strong cheekbones. Her lips called to him like a siren in the forest, a deep pink amidst the browns and greens of the pine trees. She raised one eyebrow, pulling him from his thoughts.

"I wish to catch the blackguard to make my sire and my laird proud. I want my name to be known."

"I'm sure your sire is proud that you travel with the Grant warriors. Your brother is not with us. That must mean something to him." She turned away from him to continue her search.

"Aye, I suppose you are correct." Tormod knew her statement could not be further from the truth. His brother had made sure to be at their father's home when Tormod informed his sire he'd been chosen for the journey to Edinburgh. His brother had followed his announcement with a declaration that their laird had insisted on keeping the strongest guards at home as protection against MacNiven.

In other words, he was only sending his poorly skilled warriors off to Edinburgh.

His sire had laughed.

Tormod had left the house to sleep with the warriors that night. He could still hear the echo of his brother and his sire's laughter. But Molly couldn't know that. He wanted her to think he was strong.

They reached a small clearing, and Molly pointed to one side. "You search that section and I'll search over here."

Tormod looked under bushes, between branches, and under logs, but found nothing. He pivoted, his gaze searching for Molly, only to find her in the farthest corner of the clearing with her head down and her shoulders slumped. "Molly?"

She swiped at her cheeks when she turned around, obviously embarrassed to have been caught crying.

"What is it? You have not found anything, have you?" he asked, spanning the distance between them. Shite, he hoped she hadn't found a body or anything like that.

"Nay, 'tis the problem. I've found naught. This is my sister who was kidnapped, and I've found naught. I didn't deserve to come on this trip. I'm fortunate my sire is not here to observe my failings, or he would send me back."

He brushed the tears from her face and whispered, "You have worked verra hard trying to locate your sister. I have faith in you, you must believe in yourself." Then he did the unthinkable. He leaned down and brushed his lips over hers, just the faintest of touches, but enough to make him want more. Her eyes widened, but she did not turn away from him.

She fumbled for words, enough for him to be pleased that his kiss had affected her so. "Come. Walk the periphery with me and we'll look again." Tormod's offer surprised him. Aye, he hoped to gain respect and prestige from besting MacNiven, but he needn't do it alone. The two of them both worked hard and had keen minds. Wouldn't they learn more if they processed the area together?

He'd have to trust Molly in order to invest himself in this partnership. Could he do it? Could he believe that she wasn't bent on proving herself better than him, that she was more focused on the target than on her own personal goals?

Could he do the same?

Aye, he could. Two small lassies were in the hands of a blackguard wanted by the king of the Scots. Finding them was paramount, whether he gained glory from it or not.

They moved carefully around the edge of the clearing, section by section. When they reached a large tree in the last section, Molly raced to kneel beside it.

"What is it?" Tormod stood behind her.

"The bark on this tree has been scraped away, and…just a moment." She peered closely at the base of the tree just as her mother and Gregor came up behind her.

Gwyneth knelt beside her. "What did you find? We found naught in our area so I told the guards we would join you."

"It's Jennet's, I am sure of it," Molly said, the excitement in her voice contagious.

Tormod leaned over her, "What is it? A drawing? An arrow? What?"

"I think it's the letter 'J' and…something else."

"The letter?" Tormod said, surprised. "Jennet knows how to read at her age?"

Gwyneth replied, "Brenna learned at a young age, so she insisted all of the children be taught how to read. Jennet reads her mother's medical books." She grabbed Molly's arm. "I know what it is. Your Aunt Brenna told me something before we left." Gwyneth moved Molly aside and peered even closer. "My eyes are not what they used to be, Molly, but I think 'tis a B and an S and an E."

"I agree. What do you think Tormod?"

"I cannot read. My sire never taught me, so I cannot help." Damn, but how he wished he'd learned.

Gregor leaned over his aunt's back. "You're correct, Mama. B, S, and E. I know what the B means but not the S and the E."

Gwyneth stood and glanced around the clearing. "Your mother once told me she had taught all of you that if you were ever lost in the woods to mark the trees with your initial every so often so someone could track you. So J tells us it's Jennet."

Molly jumped up. "And B tells us that Brigid is with her, and I'm guessing the S and E are the direction they're headed." She pointed in one direction. "They're going southeast—SE."

Gregor clapped his hands together. "Well done, Molly. Mama did mention that once, but I had forgotten. Southeast it is. Toward Edinburgh."

"Nice job, daughter." Gwyneth gave her a quick hug and took off behind Gregor.

"Mama, I could not have done it without Tormod," Molly called out after them. "'Twas he who pushed me to continue past my frustrations."

"Then well done, Tormod, also. Let's go head southeast."

Tormod could not believe what he'd heard. Had Molly truly gone out of her way to give him credit for something, without worrying about her own gain?

Molly spun back around to face him and said, "Aye. A clue, finally! My thanks for encouraging me." She leaned in to Tormod and pressed her lips to his briefly, but he could not stop himself. He cupped her face with both hands, and teased her with his tongue until she parted her lips with a sigh.

Tormod finally got the taste he'd wanted again, and Molly Ramsay was every bit as sweet as she had been last eve.

They'd worked well together, and he hoped it would continue. Even more, he thought he'd found someone he could trust.

That was something new, for him.

Molly had acted without thinking, shocking herself more than Tormod. She'd had every intention to pull away after giving him a quick kiss on the lips, but then she'd felt his hands on her cheeks, one thumb caressing her skin, and she'd lost all sense of reason and leaned in for more. His tongue had met her lips, and she'd parted them for him without fully realizing why, only for him to delve inside her mouth, sweeping her senses into a whirlwind. When he finally pulled back, they followed her mother back to the horses, hand in hand until they came within the others' eyesight.

She kept her head down as the heat of a blush crossed her features, hoping Tormod wouldn't notice. At the same time, she wished to shout to the heavens that she had found a clue as to her sister's location. Now they at least knew the lassies were together and both still alive. The group could not be that far ahead of them, and they would continue onward until they found another clue.

Once her mother had mounted, she turned to face the group and said, "Keep your eyes open as we travel. I suspect Jennet will leave small clues along the way. We must be diligent about finding them."

Tormod lifted Molly onto her horse, his hands giving her a soft squeeze before he stepped away to mount his own horse.

Molly's mind did somersaults as they headed southeast, bouncing from a delicious kiss, the clue her cousin had left, and the fact that she'd done something worthy of her parents' pride. That thought turned her mind toward Tormod and his sire. Something told her that he wasn't being entirely honest about his father. Mayhap he didn't want to make his sire proud for the same reasons she hoped to please Logan and Gwyneth. It could be that his sire was more like the man who'd given up her and Maggie…

A couple of hours later, she let out a squeal, shouting to her mother. "Here, Mama!" She pointed off to the side as she slipped off her horse. She'd noticed a piece of torn bark at the base of one of the trees.

Tormod was right behind her. "You've found another."

They studied the coarse markings for a few moments before her mother joined them. "I cannot read this one," her mother whispered. "'Tis too fine and blurry for me."

Molly tipped her head to the side to look at it from another angle. "I can. It's a sloppy J, and then two letters together…" She pointed to the side. "This letter she never finished. I think it would have been a B, so the other two letters must tell their direction."

She tipped her head again, and then leaned back enough to stumble and fall against Tormod, who was kneeling behind her. The force of her fall knocked him back, and his hands slipped around her waist to ensure she landed safely atop him. The heat of his body passed to hers in an instant. Her eyes widened at how pleasing it felt to be held by him. Doing her best to attempt to distract her mother from their awkward position, she whispered, "S and E. We're going southeast again."

Her mother grinned and turned back toward her horse, but not before shouting back at them. "Unhand my daughter, Moriston."

Tormod's hand released her, but then he gave her another squeeze before she rolled off of him.

Molly glanced over her shoulder at him and grinned.

She was enjoying Tormod more than she ever would have guessed.

CHAPTER ELEVEN

RANULF MACNIVEN COULDN'T HAVE BEEN more excited. True, he was not completely back to normal, but he was much better. Blasted warrior with the good aim. Ranulf would make the Ramsays pay for that, too, even though the archer was probably one of the Grant warriors. They were at their next planned stop, and when they reached another one on the morrow, they'd stay for a few days. After that, he'd head to his final destination, the place where he'd complete his dealings with the king, finish with the two lassies, and reclaim his life.

He turned to Bearchun, Shaw, Cedrica, and Lorna. "Finally, we meet up with Walrick and my other two men. Before you know it, we shall be close to Edinburgh. Everything will come to pass just as I said it would. And from now on, you will refer to me as Chief Dubh, all of you. I cannot risk anyone hearing my true name near Edinburgh."

His people sat on logs chewing on rabbit bones, and the two kidnapped lassies were leaning against a tree, their favorite activity. Why they insisted on sitting near trees was beyond him, but what could it hurt?

"What's next?" Bearchun asked. He tossed more bones over his shoulder, wiping the juice running down his chin on the sleeve of his tunic.

Ranulf paced behind him. "I'll send my messenger to the king on the morrow. 'Tis time for me to get my just due."

"And ours?" Bearchun pointed to Shaw, who sat next to him, and the lasses on the log across from him.

"And yours. I shall pay you as promised. We'll be staying less than a day's travel from Edinburgh, so we should hear back from the king quickly. We'll see how he responds to my demands."

"And what exactly are you demanding?"

"My freedom." MacNiven spun on his heel to reverse the direction of his pacing. His right hand drummed a beat on his hip as he moved. "I wish for my freedom. I've also decided to ask for my land back. He'll give me what I want—he has no choice. I'm going to meet Walrick in another hour." He grinned, anxious to have his second by his side with his conniving and devious ways. Once he conferred with Walrick, he'd make his final decision on what he wanted. His land? The chance to go across the water? Or mayhap he would just kill the girls along with everyone else. They'd put him through so much. He could have been chieftain of the Ramsay clan himself if they'd let him be.

Bearchun drew himself up from the log he had rested on. "You're leaving? Do not leave me with that wee witch."

MacNiven took several steps toward him. "Are you still allowing the lassie to get inside your head? Are you truly frightened of the wee thing?" He grinned as he taunted him. Bearchun was huge. He thought it cunning on the lassie's part to scare someone three times the size of her. Though the lass had unnerved him, she was too young to be a true witch. She was just teasing Bearchun.

Was she not?

"She's a witch. You know how I am about witches." Bearchun took two steps back as he glanced over at the lassies sitting by the tree, talking to each other and seemingly oblivious to the men.

Suddenly, Jennet turned her head to stare at Bearchun. Bearchun's hand shot out in front of him. "Tell her to stop that. Tell her, Dubh, or I'm leaving."

Cedrica got up and gave her charge a wee push. "Stop scaring the big man, wee one." She giggled as she glanced at Bearchun.

"You do not believe I'm a witch, do you?" the lassie asked her.

Cedrica snorted, looking over at the men and Lorna, who now stood next to Dubh.

"Nay, I do not."

"I curse Lorna with critters on her feet."

Her friend immediately glanced down and screamed as two otters raced across her boots and dove onto the bank of the nearby river. "Dubh, I'll not have her curse me like that. You know how I am with critters."

MacNiven could not help but laugh. He had to give it to her; Jennet knew how to spook Bearchun and the females, too. The wee lassie had no fear.

"Lassie, stop cursing Lorna and staring at my friend. You're scaring them."

"Am I?" she asked, her chin lifting until her gaze met his. God's bones, she was a bold lass for her age.

"Aye, now leave off or I'll paddle you."

He pivoted and headed back to Bearchun, feeling confident that his usual intimidating stare plus the threat would scare her enough to quiet her.

He was wrong.

"You should fear what *I* can do to *you*." Her voice crept over his shoulder, running a chill up his backbone.

His gaze widened at her suggestion. What in blazes was the lass referring to now? He turned around to glare at her, working the most demonic look he possessed. It did not work on her, though he noticed the other lass cowering behind her. At least she provided some meek entertainment for him.

"Ah, lass. You play such a game for one so young, but you see, I understand lassies of your kind. You are the daughter of a healer. 'Tis not possible for you to hurt someone." Life had taught him that was true.

"Shut her up, Dubh. I do not like her." Bearchun's voice echoed through the trees.

Jennet twisted her lips into an odd pucker, as though her mind were busy conniving. "I must admit that you are correct. However, since I am a medical expert, I must do research to determine if my hypotheses are true. I have a couple of experiments planned for this trip. Would you like to know more about them?"

"Hush!" MacNiven picked her up and shook her. "You have my men frightened to their toes. You cannot hurt me, so end your foolishness."

She glanced down at him and whispered, "My thanks for moving me so close to your face. 'Twill help me when I carry out my research."

"Your words do not frighten me, lass. I am Chief Dubh. You need to fear me. I can throw you over the embankment into the ice cold water and leave you to die." He shook her again just for good measure.

He expected to see fear in her gaze when he finished, but it was not what he found. Her gaze had only narrowed. How had one so young become so bold?

"You will not throw me over an embankment until you have gained whatever you hope to exchange for our safe return. If you kill me now, you'll have naught to bargain with. Just to forewarn you, when you awaken tomorrow and you cannot see, 'tis only part of my experiment."

"What experiment?" The lass talked in circles sometimes. He had no idea what she intended. Hellfire, but she was a clever one.

"Now that I've gotten a closer look, I know exactly how I'll do it."

"Do what?" He brought her face close to his, and as soon as he did, she broke into a wide grin.

"I plan to sew your eyes shut when you're sleeping. I've always wanted to see how fine the stitches would need to be."

His reaction was to toss the lass away from him, and she fell to the ground with an oomph. But she recovered quickly and ran over to her spot by the tree. He wiped his hand across his mouth as he watched her retreat. He'd never met anyone like her. The lass had the devil inside her. Sew his eyes shut? He stepped back as he imagined awakening in such a state, his arms pulling in closer to his body.

Bearchun barked behind him. "Do you not see? She's evil, I tell you. She's the devil. Kill her and keep the other to bargain with the king."

MacNiven's mind continued to reel until a lad on horseback rode into camp. "Chief, we've got trouble and it's coming our way."

He gave his attention to the lad. "What is it, Ros?"

"I've been patrolling to see what's in the area, just as you bade me to do. There's a group of Ramsays coming this way, some with bows. I think the ballocks lady is with them."

"Gwyneth Ramsay?" God's teeth, they'd have to be careful.

"How in hell has she found us? This spot is a good distance off the regular track. I do not understand."

"I listened to them from the tree as they passed. Apparently, someone has been marking the trees with messages, telling them where you are headed."

"What? 'Tis impossible. Two lassies could not leave..." He halted mid-sentence and marched over to the tree, lifting Jennet away from it. He saw the etchings in the bark at the base of the tree.

"You wee bitch!" He tossed her off to the side, then turned to his men. "Gather your things. We head to our next destination early. The bitch gave us away." Jennet ran off to another tree, away from the men.

Shaw walked over to the tree to look at Jennet's etchings. "I know not what anyone could get from those etchings. 'Tis not a picture of aught. What does it mean?"

"Those are letters, you idiot," Ranulf bellowed. "She's leaving directions. Can you not read? SE...southeast, which is exactly where we are headed next, or where we *were* headed next. I've decided to change it now. Shaw, hide those etchings so no one can see them."

Spinning around in a circle, he searched for the troublemakers. Jennet was sitting against a distant tree, facing him with her hands demurely behind her back. This time, he'd frighten the lass until she cried. He picked Brigid up and held her in front of Jennet and roared. "I should kill her for all the trouble you've caused."

Brigid began to wail, and Bearchun bellowed, "Stop that crying. I hate crying."

Jennet leaned close to Ranulf. "Do not forget that I am a witch. And if you hurt her at all, mayhap I'll sew your tongue to your upper lip after I finish sewing your eyes."

He dropped Brigid to the ground and picked Jennet up, tossing her onto his horse. "I do not believe a word of what you say. We're leaving. Shaw, the wee wailer rides with you. We must go immediately."

The Ramsay bitch was starting to frighten him, and she'd outsmarted all of them with her messages. Hell, but his stomach had turned queasy at the thought of her foolish threats.

He'd keep a better eye on her from now on.

As long as he was still able to open them.

Tormod tugged on the reins of his horse, pulling his mount up short. He'd heard Molly yell something about another spot marked by Jennet. He shook his head as he thought about how intelligent Molly and her wee cousin were, how they often left him feeling inadequate. He had to admit that before this trip, he'd not known many women well other than his brother's wife. His time was mostly spent at the lists. True, he'd heard many stories about Maddie Grant, but he'd never heard of women as strong as Molly or Ashlyn, or even Molly's mother. The Highlands were full of tales about Gwyneth of Ramsay, but even the tales did not do her justice. She had a calm strength rarely seen in men or women.

Molly's insight and logic amazed him, and Jennet, why she was just beyond belief. If he told anyone what she'd done, they'd not believe him. The lass had been kidnapped by a true blackguard, but she'd kept her wits about her. Not many would have stayed as strong under those same circumstances.

Molly hopped off her horse and ran to look at the base of a tree, so he jumped down after her. The etchings on the raw spot on this tree trunk weren't done as carefully as the others had been. Gregor joined them, though the guards stayed on their horses.

"Mama?" Molly yelled to her mother as she tipped her head to see the etchings from a different angle.

Gwyneth appeared next to Molly, her hand on one of her daughter's shoulders. "What is it? What does it say?"

"I cannot read it," Molly said. "I don't think she finished it."

Gregor looked and declared, "That is verra confusing. I know not what she means with that etching."

Tormod leaned down to peer at it more closely, then stood up, rubbing his hands on his tartan. "This one is much different from the others. Are you sure it's from Jennet? Mayhap 'tis just animal scratchings. Red squirrels digging for food."

"How I wish I could see the fine details to help you," Gwyneth said, "but alas, I cannot. My eyes fail me up close. If I only could see through your young eyes. Describe it to me, please?"

Molly stared at it again, running her fingers across the bark.

Tormod was anxious for her assessment, but he could tell she needed time to process what she was seeing. Finally, she stood and pivoted toward them.

"I believe someone scratched over what Jennet was working on."

"MacNiven?" Tormod's eyes widened at the implications.

"Aye. I think someone discovered what she was doing and tried to erase the clues she'd left us."

Gwyneth's hand shook as she brushed a hair back from her face. "Can you make out the message?"

"Nay. Just the J." Molly reached for her mother's hand. "Mama, we'll find Brigid. We will. Mayhap Papa has already found her."

"I know." Gwyneth's voice came out in the barest of whispers.

The great Gwyneth Ramsay, spy for the Scottish Crown, renowned archer in all of England, probably one of the strongest women he'd ever seen, had been undone by the thought of what that daft man might do to her youngest daughter. Tormod's hands came to rest on his hips as he began to pace the area. Perhaps there was another clue they had all missed.

"Even if we could determine Jennet's etchings," Gwyneth said, still speaking softly. "I do not know that I would trust it. Once discovered, MacNiven likely changed his plans."

Tormod could not find anything else in the area, so moved back to the tree. He ran his hand across it as Molly had done. "I believe 'tis another squiggly line as before."

"You mean an S?"

Tormod shrugged. "I know not…I cannot read, but it looks similar to the other etchings." He picked up a stick and traced a shadow in the dirt. "Much like this."

"I agree with you there," Molly said. "I think it could be an S, but I thought there might be something else next to it, mayhap an E, confirming we are following the correct path."

Gregor leaned over to look again. "I cannot make any sense of that." He moved away to allow the others a closer look.

"What do you think, Lady Ramsay?" Tormod asked.

"Jennet is sending us to Edinburgh."

Molly paced the small area, then suddenly bolted over to another tree.

"What is it?" Tormod asked as he followed her to the tree off to the side.

"There. Look, 'tis just barely an etching. But I do believe it could be another message." She knelt down next to the tree, ripping brown weeds away from the tree to give herself better access.

"What is it?" Gwyneth stood back, wringing her hands. "Tell me 'tis something better than what we have."

Molly's gaze narrowed as she stared at the new set of carvings she'd found. "I'm not sure. 'Tis not as carefully done as before."

"Mayhap she tried to give us another clue after she was discovered because MacNiven had changed his plan."

"It makes sense," Molly said, "especially if he tried to cover up her other message. This one…I just cannot be sure." She hesitated, but then sat back on her heels. "It could be an N or a W that she was not able to finish. What would be to the west? It's slanted as though she were in a hurry."

Gwyneth thought for a moment. "N would indicate he was returning to Perthshire and his castle. W could indicate he was heading more toward the Buchans, or to some unknown place. I believe he has found a new hiding place. He'd be wise to find a place we are unaware of, something well hidden. No one would expect him to go west."

Molly held her head. "So we now have three choices? Southeast to Edinburgh, north to MacNiven's castle, or west to an undetermined location? But we would have no assistance if we head north or west. If we go to Edinburgh, we can find Da and see what he has learned."

"I say to Edinburgh," Gwyneth said. "We'll see if we can locate your sire. He may have new information."

"Aye, I agree," Gregor said. "Let's move out."

Molly nodded. "We go southeast."

Tormod set his feet apart and crossed his arms in front of him, ready for his battle. Here was his chance. He'd analyzed it all in his head, and was certain the blackguard would head for his land. Now, he only had to convince them. "I disagree. I say we head to MacNiven's castle. The man is headed home. He was planning to go to Edinburgh at first. He could get a message to the king faster that way. But they discovered Jennet's etchings, erased them, and changed their plans. Now they're headed north to his land."

Molly swung to face him. "Nay, we have already decided. Three to one voice. We go to Edinburgh."

"I'll add another thought. We were not far from them. Someone saw us coming, and MacNiven is running from us, running scared. We are the reason he changed plans, us and Jennet."

Molly gave him a look he could not interpret, but she did not stand up for him. She only shrugged her shoulders.

Tormod tapped his foot on the ground. "We're making a huge mistake."

CHAPTER TWELVE

MOLLY LOOKED FROM HER MOTHER to Tormod and then to Gregor, unsure of what to say. Was Tormod correct? Would they be making a huge mistake if they went to Edinburgh?

Gwyneth placed her hands on her daughter's shoulders. "Molly, I want you to go back and look at the etchings again. You are the only one who can judge them properly. I cannot see it, Tormod cannot read, and Gregor is not the best at his letters, though I'd like him to take another look. Was Jennet trying to tell us to go in a different direction, and if so, which way?"

Molly's stomach somersaulted at least five times before she could force herself to walk over to the tree to take another look.

Gregor eventually joined her, peering over her shoulder. "I do not see what you see. I say Edinburgh."

Her mother said. "Molly, if you strongly believe that Tormod is correct, please say so."

The decision was hers—and hers alone.

"Take your time. 'Tis more important that you are correct than that you do it fast." Tormod's blue eyes burned into hers. He believed in her, though she did not understand why when her mother stood not far from her. Did he not know her mother was the best spy and archer—best female, really—in all the land?

Molly did her best to focus on the task at hand. True, it could be an N indicating north, but it could also be part of a W... Or it could be nothing at all. What if the mark had not been made by Jennet at all? What if it had been made by Brigid, imitating her cousin? Brigid did not know her letters as well as Jennet did. She rubbed her forehead, wishing she could make a decision.

The reality was she could not. She did not trust her own judgment enough. They needed to find her father, see what he thought, see where they should go next. Her sire could eliminate the doubt in her mind. He made his decisions quickly, without hesitation, something she could not do.

She stood and faced her mother, her hands behind her back. "Mama, I cannot be sure. I think it may be an N, but it is quite crooked. Mayhap we should go see Da, see what he thinks..."

"Molly." Tormod's voice was thick with exasperation. "Trust your instincts. You have good judgment. Take another look and tell us what you think. Do not be afraid to make a decision."

"Aye, just tell us what you see, and we'll go that way." The pain in her mother's face broke her heart. She considered her options again, but came up with the same answer.

She could not do it. Her mother or father had always made the decisions. She just could not be sure what Jennet had intended.

Her shoulders slumped and she whispered, "I cannot tell for sure. I say we go to Edinburgh."

Tormod shook his head and she turned away, not wanting to see his disappointment. He did not understand the reasoning behind her decision.

"You are capable of making the right decision, lass," Tormod said. "Do the right thing. Your sister's life is at stake."

And what if she was wrong? What if they went north and her sister had been taken west or southeast toward Edinburgh? Then it would be entirely her fault. She could not take that risk. It would be best to meet up with her sire and the others. They could all help her think her way through this situation.

"Edinburgh," Molly said to her mother. "We must find Da."

Gwyneth mounted her horse in one smooth movement. "Edinburgh is where we go. Mount up all."

Molly mounted, but she could feel the anger emanating from Tormod. He truly believed they should head north. Mayhap he was even angry with her for not choosing to side with him. He didn't understand that she couldn't risk any more harm to her sister. She would leave the decision making to her parents once they made it to Edinburgh. They did not have much farther to go. He finally climbed onto his horse and flicked his reins to follow them out, though he would not look at her.

Little passed between them as they traveled. Sundown was almost upon them when they reached the outskirts of the burgh. Molly's mother pointed off in a distance toward the clearing they often used as a meeting place. It was about an hour from the burgh, far enough that they wouldn't be bothered.

Her mother held her hand up as they reached the clearing and then gave a bird call a few times to see if Logan would appear. Just as they'd hoped, Molly's sire bolted out of the clearing on horseback, his face hopeful. "Well? Did you find our lasses?"

Molly's mother shook her head. "Nay. We followed them through the forest. Jennet was quite clever about leaving us clues, but we think she's been discovered." Once they'd both dismounted and moved into the clearing in front of the cave, Gwyneth gave him the rest of their information. Molly stood off to the side, anxious to hear what her father had to say.

Her heart broke into several pieces as she listened. Her father had found naught more than they had, in fact, he'd encountered no clues at all. He'd spoken to the king, who'd not yet heard any demands from MacNiven.

"What did King Alexander say?" her mother asked her father.

"He said he guessed MacNiven would ask to be pardoned, and he said he would grant it. Once the girls are in our hands, we can go after MacNiven, wherever he is." Her father closed his eyes and clenched his fists, a heavy breath sneaking through his pursed lips.

Molly could see how this entire event had rankled her sire, something she rarely saw.

"Unless he goes off on a ship or something," Jamie added. "If he has the coin, he could pay to cross the sea."

"Then I'll pray for a bad storm and hope his ship goes down. I'll not chase after him if he leaves England. I know our king says to leave him and wait for his demands, but I'll not stand around waiting for a blackguard to run this and tell us what to do. He's got my daughter and my niece. Whether now or after he makes his demands, I'll find him and kill him with my bare hands," Molly's father said, wrapping his arm around Gwyneth and pulling her close to him so she could rest her head on his shoulder.

"We shall rest this night and leave on the morrow," Molly's father said.

"Think on it. We should probably divide up again, some of can head to Edinburgh and the rest can go north or west. We have decisions to make."

Snow had fallen, which would help them trail the men, but it meant the ground would turn even colder. Molly could see her breath as she finally stood and headed out to the woods to take care of her needs. Disappointed her sire hadn't uncovered more, she reviewed all in her mind, hoping to think of something she'd missed.

When she headed back to the cave, she started when Tormod stepped out from behind a bush in front of her. He took her hand and pulled her away from the cave. The heat of his hand warmed hers through her gloves, warmed her all the way to her core, and she took an unintentional step closer to him.

When he stopped, she almost bumped into him. He spun around and glared at her. "Why do you not trust your instincts?"

Molly, totally puzzled, shook her head, but no words came out.

"You think Jennet wrote an N, but you would not tell your mother. Why not?"

"I...you do not understand..." She fumbled for words, not sure how to explain what had been in her head. He was right—she *had* thought it was an N, but how could she make him understand that what she thought did not matter? "Because I was not sure..."

"You were. I could see it in your hands, the way you traced the letter. The problem is that you do not believe in yourself. Why not?"

"Because...my parents are spies for the Crown. You know that. Their judgment is much better than mine. I am just an adopted English girl who was lucky to be chosen by them."

"What? What does that have to do with your judgment? Besides, you are as Scottish as I am now."

"Aye. I was English. I am Scottish now. I renounced my birth parents. Logan and Gwyneth Ramsay are my parents." The heat of his breath stroked her skin, causing her to flush in more places than she would have thought possible. She stood outside in winter, bundled up in leggings, a tunic, and a plaid over her shoulders, and it was cold enough to see her breath, but she felt warm whenever she was around Tormod.

"So you were English. You're Scottish now, but do not denigrate yourself. You are a mighty intelligent lass. Tell them what you think. Tell your sire what you truly believe."

Molly stared into his deep blue eyes, wondering how anyone could stand this close to him and keep their focus. Her tongue seemed tied into a knot, and her thoughts were muddled and foolish. She dared not put voice to any of them or she'd embarrass herself.

A voice echoed from behind her. "Tell your sire what?" Her father stood next to them.

Tormod dropped her hand but continued to stare at her. "Go ahead. Tell him."

Molly looked up at Tormod, willing her mind to function and her tongue to untie so she could speak to her father.

"Molly?"

She turned to her sire. "Papa, I…" She cleared her throat and stared at the ground.

Her father grasped her chin, forcing her gaze to meet his. "Molly, tell me what you believe. I'd like your thoughts please. Tell me all and do not leave aught out. I understand you do not like to speak in front of an audience, but 'tis only me and Tormod."

Her sire dropped his hand from her chin, and she nodded. "Aunt Brenna taught all of her bairns that if they were ever stolen away, they needed to leave clues to help you and Mama find them. She suggested carving letters into trees—the first letter in their name and the direction they were traveling."

"Aye, Mama told us that. You found J and B for Jennet and Brigid. And SE for southeast. Go on."

She glanced at Tormod, and the look on his face gave her courage. "The last etching was a bit of a mess. I believe her captors discovered what she was doing, noticed the SE and tried to scratch it out. When they did that, I think Jennet snuck over to another tree and tried to send a new message about their destination, mayhap because MacNiven changed his mind, but she tried to hide it, mayhap with her back to the tree. She would have been more careful after being discovered. It wasn't as neat as the letters Jennet had carved before."

"And what do you think she wrote?"

"An N for north. We talked about how it could be a W that wasn't finished, but if she was writing behind her back, the letter would be upside down, and an N upside down would appear to us as an N." It was the first time she'd shared that last part aloud.

"What hand does she write with?"

"Her right."

Her sire took a twig and held it behind his back, then leaned over so he could write in the dirt. He spun around to see the letter and said, "Right you are. Jennet is a bright lass; she would know that. They've gone north." He gave her a hug and ran back toward the cave, shouting over his shoulder, "Well done, Molly. Next time believe in yourself."

Tormod reached for her hand and cocooned it inside his, a broad smile on his face.

"Moriston, unhand my daughter if you wish to live," Logan bellowed.

Tormod dropped her hand as though a blazing fire had erupted from her.

"Damn, he's quick." He peered after her sire. "But he's right. You must believe in yourself."

CHAPTER THIRTEEN

RANULF MACNIVEN SMILED WHEN HIS castle came into view. Home. He'd thought he'd never see his land again. Many had deserted him after he was sentenced to the hangman's noose, but his most devoted men had stayed, believing he'd find a way back. Looking at his keep and his land wrenched his emotions more than he'd expected. Aye, he'd considered going to the south of England, getting on a boat and sailing the seas, but standing here in front of his own gates made him a bit melancholy.

When he'd left, he'd sworn to return, and he had. But where did he belong?

He stopped his horse by the gates, a wide smile bursting across his face. Dying to see who had stayed loyal to him, he bellowed, "Open up. I'm back!"

His declaration was met with a few cheers as the portcullis was raised. Some men he recognized hung over the curtain wall, shouting their greetings to him. "Earc, Ninean, you're still here?"

"Och," Ninean replied. "We'd not leave you. We knew if naught else, your rotten spirit would be back to haunt the place."

"Aye, and we had to be here to see it," Earc chuckled.

"Good to see you, Chief," Ninean said with a smirk. "I win the wager. I was sure your sorry hide would return to these parts, cussing and spitting. I knew I'd live to see it. Toss up your coins, lads, Chief MacNiven made it."

Walrick pulled his horse up alongside MacNiven. "He goes by Dubh now. 'Tis the way he wishes to be addressed."

"Chief Dubh is my latest name, 'tis true, and I prefer it to the old. I've been reinvented and rejuvenated, and I'm intent on bringing us back to our rightful place as the strongest clan in the Highlands." He passed through the gate and dismounted to greet his comrades, leaving Jennet still on the horse.

"Who are the wee lassies?" Earc said, his smile leaving his face. "And the other men you brought?"

Shaw came from the rear of the group of warriors, Brigid still crying in front of him.

"Dubh, make her stop," Bearchun bellowed, "or I swear I'm leaving as soon as he dumps her off his horse."

Jennet slid off her horse and raced over to Brigid. "I'll take her. If she's with me, she'll stay quiet."

Earc shoved Jennet's hands away and reached for Brigid. "A wee lassie, and a pretty one at that. I'll take her."

Jennet swung at him. "Leave her be!"

Brigid screamed louder the minute Earc touched her. Tears flowed in rivers down her face and her entire body shook. Just the kind of fear Ranulf loved to see in his subordinates.

Laughing, Earc ran his hands across her bottom. He shoved his face in front of Brigid's as he held her in the air, a wide, feral grin on his face. "I'll swat your arse or kiss your arse, which one will it be, lassie?"

Jennet lunged for Shaw's dagger. Fool that he was, he let her grab ahold of it. Thrusting it out in front of her, she stepped back from all the men. "Let her go or I'll curse you, one at a time."

Ros guffawed. "Chief, you grabbed a feisty one this time. I like her. She'll be fun to break."

Bearchun broke away from them, sweat pouring down his face. "Make her stop, Dubh. You promised. I'll not be threatened by the wee witch."

"He's correct," Jennet screeched. "I am a witch in a lassie's body, and I'll drop you to the ground one at a time, without even touching you." She stepped back, one foot at a time, slowing the process as she pointed the dagger at each of them in turn. "Shall I curse you?" she pointed to Ros, who had suddenly turned serious and was staring at her as though she had two heads.

"Or you?" She pointed to Earc, then Ninean. "Or mayhap you? Would you like to drop to the ground and stop breathing?"

"Of what does she speak, Chief?" Ninean said. "She's spooking me a bit. I do not like her ways. She has wild eyes. 'Tis true? She's a witch?"

"Aye, she's a witch," Bearchun bellowed. "Beware her curses!"

MacNiven barked, "Nay, she's not a witch, but she's verra good at frightening huge men like Bearchun." Though he noticed Cedrica and Lorna still hid behind him, unwilling to go near the lasses unless ordered.

Jennet spun and pointed to him. "Shall I drop you, Dubh?"

Brigid screamed louder, for Earc was holding her closer against his body.

"Leave us be, or I swear I'll curse you," Jennet threatened again.

MacNiven laughed, a rumbling laugh that started in his belly and carried through his entire body. Shite, the lass was almost as conniving as he was. Almost. He'd show her. She jumped back when he reached for her, but not before cutting his hand.

When she connected with his flesh, she hollered, "*Mo mhallachd ort.*"

Bearchun screeched, "She cursed you!"

He yelled, "You wee bitch!" Blood was trickling down his arm and into his sleeve.

She spun around to face Bearchun, who'd gone as pale as bed linens, and MacNiven took the opportunity to wipe the blood away. The bitch had actually wounded him, and he could not allow the others to see his weakness.

Apparently, the wee witch was not finished. Before he could stop her, she looked at Bearchun and, with the flick of her wrist, drew the knife across the back of her hand. Holding it up to his face, she said, "I curse you, Bearchun. *Mo mhallachd ort.* You are the first."

Bearchun took one look at the blood trailing down her hand and crumpled to the ground, his eyes closed.

"Who wishes to be cursed next?" She held the dagger out in front of her as the men stared at Bearchun in shock, stepping back as if she possessed an invincible power.

Shaw pointed to her. "She's done it before. I've seen her. She *is* a witch."

MacNiven shoved the toe of his boot against Bearchun's belly. "Get up. 'Tis not amusing to me. Get up, you lazy arse." Bearchun did not even flinch.

"Let her go or you're next." She pointed her dagger at Earc, who needed no other warning to drop Brigid to the ground. The wee lassie raced over to hide behind Jennet, sniffling and hugging her cousin from behind.

MacNiven held his hands up. "Have it your way. I still hold the daughter of Logan Ramsay and the sister of Torrian Ramsay, both my enemies." He turned to the rest of the group, including Bearchun, who still lay unmoving on the ground. "If any of you touch either lass, you'll have to deal with me."

"Or be cursed by me," Jennet whispered.

He pivoted to glare to her. "Stop spooking my guards. You'll bide your tongue. The two of you shall stay in my solar off the hall so you'll not be a temptation to my men. I'll bring you food and water, but only if you agree to stop cursing everyone. Cedrica and Lorna will sit outside your door to make sure you stay put."

Jennet tucked the dagger into the folds of her skirt and then hugged Brigid. Finally, as if coming to a decision, she nodded. "Aye, if you'll leave us be. Send a message to Logan Ramsay. You'll get what you want." She spun on her heel and marched toward the great hall.

"Keep her far away from me," Ros whispered. "I do not like wee witches. Mayhap she is a black faerie."

MacNiven grumbled to himself as he followed the lassies up the stairs to the great hall. He glanced over his shoulder at Bearchun, shaking his head. The big lout had collapsed faster than a ripe old warrior with a sword in his belly.

Focus. He needed to focus on his plan. He had to get two messages out, one to the king, and one to the other person he needed most. For now, he'd forget about the wee lassies since he did not yet need them.

He had to forget about them, because if he thought much about the lass, she'd scare every wiry hair from his head.

Without a doubt, she was a witch, and he'd be wise to be careful around her.

CHAPTER FOURTEEN

MOLLY STARED AT THE BLUE eyes locked on hers.
Tormod repeated himself. "Why do you not believe in your-self? You must speak what you saw, not be timid."

"I am not timid, I am but careful." She wrapped her arms around herself.

Tormod tucked a lock of her hair behind her ear. "Why? You were raised by the strongest woman in all of England. You must have learned from her. Or are you afraid of your own mother?"

"Nay, I am not afraid of her. I love my mother. She was the first one to love…well…my English mother…mayhap…other than Maggie."

He chucked her under the chin. "You were raised by the great Ram-say clan. Your parents are spies for the Crown, spies who have done so much for the Scots. We were not all fortunate enough to have such an opportunity."

Molly had had enough. Enough of his prodding and judging and pushing. Aye, she could tell he'd had a hard time of it, too, but she would not let him judge her. He thought her too timid? She'd tell him exactly what her life had been like. "And neither was I. I was not raised by the best until almost half my childhood was over.

"I was raised by a man who hated girls. Do you know what he did? I had six brothers and two sisters. My sire said he could no longer feed so many mouths, so he decided to give one of us away. My brothers each ate twice as much as I did. In fact, I ate the least of anyone in the family. But he chose to give me away. My mother insisted I not go

alone and sent Maggie with me. He could have given one of my brothers away, and it would have had the same effect, but he gave two lasses
away. Why? Because he thought we were useless. In fact, after he made
the arrangement, he thought to give my other sister away, too, but he
decided to keep one lass to assist my mother with the household chores
and because my mother begged him not to give all of us away."

"But then you were adopted by the Ramsays. Logan Ramsay has
more respect for women than anyone I know. It was the best thing that
could have happened."

"Aye, but at first I wasn't adopted by the Ramsays. We were sold to
an English family, a nasty woman who used the switch on us. Her son
liked to touch girls in ways I did not like." Her voice cracked and a tear
slid down her cheek.

"Molly, I'm sorry. I did not know." He brushed away her tears, and
when she looked into her eyes, she saw that he meant it. "I understand
what 'tis like to feel unloved. My sire always preferred my brother. Lyall
could never make a mistake. My sire considered everything he did to be
better than everything I did—and he made sure I knew it."

"But he did not give you away! How would that feel to you?" She
knew her face had turned red with anger, but she did not care. How she
hated her sire for what he'd done to her and Maggie.

"It could have been better for me. Once you were with the Ramsays,
your life improved. You've had instruction from the best of the best.
Love."

"I know, I know that." Molly's face fell into her hands. No one knew
her good fortune better than she did. The Ramsays had been a blessing
she hadn't dared hope for.

"Then why did you not tell your mother what you thought? Why did
you question yourself?"

"Because I do not wish to be given away again!" She shoved at Tormod's shoulders as her innermost feelings finally came out. "If I'm
wrong, mayhap my sire would give me away. I would die if that ever
happened."

"Lass, your parents would never give you away. I'd never believe that
of them. 'Twill not happen." He ran his hand down her arm in an
attempt to comfort her.

"What if Brigid died because of me? If we went north and she was
west, it could happen. There would be no one to blame but me! They
would hate me." She collapsed into his arms and he wrapped his arms

around her as sobs wracked her body.

"It was awful when the English lad looked at me that way. Once he touched me and said I was not yet ready. I hated him...I...I wished to hurt him. Fortunately, Gwyneth Ramsay came upon me after I was beaten with a switch at his mother's orders. She found me tethered to a tree out in the cold. It hurt so much, and Gwyneth just stole me away, threatening to hurt them both if they tried to reclaim me. She even went back for Maggie. I love them so much. I could not bear to be apart from them. I know not what would happen to me."

Tormod's hand rubbed her back through the plaid. He kissed her cheek and whispered, "Forgive me. I had no idea. 'Tis worse than my situation. I understand your fear, but you need not worry. You *are* a Ramsay, and your family will never give you up."

When her tears slowed, he cupped her cheeks and kissed her with the gentlest touch possible. She clutched his tunic, sighing at the taste of his lips, wanting more. His tongue swept inside her mouth, and she tentatively touched it with hers. He groaned, and she guessed that to be a good thing, so she continued, delving her tongue into his mouth until she lost all ability to think, her breath coming out in short pants. His hands moved down to cup her backside and pull her closer. Her breasts tightened, feeling as if they were about to burst. What was happening to her?

He stopped abruptly and set her apart from him. "Your father's warning is still fresh in my mind."

She nodded, mostly because that was all she was capable of doing. Tormod took her hand and led her back to the cave, only letting go at the last possible moment. Before they parted, he kissed her cheek and said, "Believe in yourself and your parents."

And those simple words were enough to lift her heart and raise her spirits.

The next morn, Jamie, Coll, Braden, Gavin, and Gregor headed to Edinburgh to update the king, while Molly's mother and father, Sorcha, Torrian, Kyle, and Tormod all headed north with her. She and Tormod kept their distance, but he glanced her way often enough to make her hopeful.

She'd made a fool of herself in front of him, yet he did not seem to mind. Mayhap when this was all over, Tormod would wish to court her.

Except he was a Grant warrior and would be returning to Grant land. It was better if she did not set her hopes too high—she'd seen what a

broken heart could do to a lass, and she wanted no part in it. And yet...
Being around Tormod, even thinking about him, made her feel happy
in a way she'd never expected to feel. She did not converse much in
their travels because she was too lost in her mixed up feelings. She knew
not what to make of them, and all the thinking and analyzing in the
world would not help her. There was no logic to any of it.

When they had almost reached MacNiven land, her sire held his arm
up, stopping them. They had also brought twenty guards with them—a
protective measure in case a battle broke out. "Settle here. Gwyneth and
I will ride ahead to determine if anyone is here or if we need to retrace
our path. No one else is to move. Torrian, you're in charge."

They were gone more than an hour, and Molly was so nervous she
didn't know what to do. Torrian finally led them over to a small area
and pointed to the trees in the distance. "Practice, Molly. 'Twill keep
you busy. Tormod, are you better with your bow or your sword?"

"Better with my sword, my lord, but I've been practicing with my
bow."

Torrian snorted. "There's no lord here. Call me Torrian. Go ahead
and practice with your bow. No swords, 'tis too loud. We are quite a
distance away from the castle, but I will not take any chances. He may
have guards in the periphery." He took his own bow and quiver off his
horse.

Kyle came over and said, "I'll join you. Waiting is the part of battling I
hate most. Practicing will help pass the time, though I'll take swordplay
on any field over my bow."

It wasn't long before they all were asking Molly and Sorcha for pointers.

Kyle stood to the back, his arms crossed, observing each of them.
Normally, Kyle trained Torrian's warriors so Molly was interested to
hear what Kyle thought of Tormod's skills. At one point Kyle whistled.
"Torrian, I oft thought you were the best of us, but Molly can outshoot
you. Sorcha's also good, but not as sharp as Molly. She has a dead eye."

Torrian scowled at his best friend. "Molly has always been the best of
our *siol*. Though Ashlyn has gotten better and better."

Molly spoke while she pulled her bow back, aiming for another tree.
"Ashlyn now has the reputation we've all hoped for. She's the lass who
hit the hunted man."

Kyle quirked a brow at her. "All of us? I'm not so sure about that,
Molly."

Molly glanced from Torrian to Tormod to Kyle. "Nay? You have not wished it was you who hit the blackguard?"

"I have," Tormod replied as the other two shook their heads.

Molly rolled her eyes at Kyle and Torrian. "You two are in love. 'Tis the only reason you do not care."

Sorcha grinned. "Aye, they are besotted, just as I wish to be. Only, I have not found the right lad yet. Molly, you continue to shoot your arrows at the blackguards; I'll shoot love arrows at the lads. But you must free our sisters first." Sorcha's shoulders slumped, as though the reality of their troubles had just come back to her.

"We do care that MacNiven was hit and hope more than aught that the villain is caught and pays for his crimes, but we do not care who the shooter is. Just find the bastard. If you and Molly would find yourselves lads," Torrian said, "mayhap you'd understand why we have priorities." He stood back and watched Tormod shoot three arrows. "You are not bad either." Then he tipped his head toward Tormod, looking at Molly. "Cousin, why do you not get to know Tormod a wee bit better."

Molly dropped her bow, frowning at Torrian, who laughed and announced, "I think I just hit a different mark."

A noise stopped them all in their tracks, and they turned to see Logan and Gwyneth had returned. Molly hurried over to them, her heart fluttering with fear when her sire raced over to help her mother down from her horse.

"Mama?" Molly moved closer to them, Sorcha following directly behind her.

Gwyneth winced as Logan helped her over to a log. "Sit and I'll remove your boot to see what's wrong," he said.

"Logan, there's no need. I twisted my ankle. I just need to rest it." As soon as she sat on the log, her hands moved to her ankle.

Logan pushed them aside. "I'll do it. Lean back and try to relax."

She did, but Molly could see the pain twisting her features. Her hands curled into fists, her jaw clenched, and her eyes squeezed shut as he removed the boot. "Gwynie, 'tis quite swollen. It could be broken."

"Nay, I think not. It turned in a hole in the ground, causing me to lose my balance. There wasn't the snap of a breaking bone." He touched the side of her ankle and her mother gasped. "Please, not there, Logan. 'Tis too painful."

Molly could not believe her eyes. Her mother had always been invincible, yet here she was unable to get up without wincing in pain, unable to…

Gads, but her mother would not be able to travel to the castle.

As if her mother had overheard her thoughts, she said, "I'm of no use to you now. I'm grounded."

Logan squeezed her hand and kissed her cheek. "You still have that clever mind of yours, do you not? My Gwynie can strategize better than most. You'll just not be in the front lines as you are used to."

But then who would take her place?

CHAPTER FIFTEEN

TORMOD, STILL IN A DAZE after seeing the great Gwyneth Ramsay sidelined with an injury, followed Logan and the others into the next field, leaving Gwyneth, Molly, and Sorcha behind with four guards to protect them. He sensed that Logan wished to leave the lassies alone with their mother for a short time.

Torrian spoke before they stopped. "Enough holding your information inside. Are they here? Is MacNiven in his castle?"

Tormod felt anxious for the answers. Had he and Molly been correct, or had they sent everyone in the wrong direction?

Logan crossed his arms and stood in a wide stance, waiting for them to form a group in front of him. "Aye, MacNiven is here," he said at last. "The only others I recognized were Bearchun and Shaw, though Bearchun has been taken ill. He was carried inside the stables."

"Are you sure he's not dead?" Kyle asked.

"Nay, I could still hear his mouth running wild. I look forward to the chance to put my fist in that mouth, or—better yet—my boot. I warned my brother about him."

"And Jennet and Brigid?" Torrian asked.

Logan dropped his head to stare at the ground, pausing as he dug the toe of his boot into the wet grass. "We did not find them, though we did not make it into the great hall. We only watched from afar. Once Gwynie hurt her ankle, I was not willing to go any closer, no matter what she wished to do. Our count was near thirty guards, and I do not think we saw all of them, so let's assume his numbers are around fifty."

Torrian started to pace. "If MacNiven's there along with Bearchun, then the lassies must be hidden in the keep somewhere. We will have to plan carefully to make sure they are not hurt when we attack."

Tormod wondered who would be giving the orders. While Torrian was the chieftain of the Ramsays, Logan was his uncle, Brigid's sire, and a spy for the Crown.

"They were all talking about some witch they're afraid of, but we could not determine who it was."

Tormod stiffened. "A witch? Did that come from Bearchun or Shaw?"

"Aye, Bearchun swore repeatedly about some witch who'd cursed him. Does that mean anything to you?" His gaze searched the group before returning to Tormod. "If it does, speak up, Moriston."

"In the great hall, Jamie had just introduced us to Jennet and Brigid when Bearchun came along and cursed Jennet as a witch. She told us something about an experiment she'd run on the lout. He fainted whenever he saw blood, and her sire was worried he'd fall unconscious in the middle of battle." He glanced around at the others, but no one else knew of what he spoke. Then it dawned on him. "Molly would know, possibly."

"Nay, she would not. She was with us in Edinburgh. Torrian? What do you know of this?"

Torrian rubbed his chin. "I recall a time when Jennet brought out a container of red liquid to see if it would make Bearchun faint, and he fell to the ground. He was furious when he awakened. But he had no ill effects from it." His hands moved to his hips. "He must have been referring to my sister. She must be this witch they were talking about. What else did they say?"

Logan replied, "Just that the witch was being kept in a chamber inside, and someone else was expected to arrive. That was about the time Gwynie fell."

"That tells us that Jennet is there, probably with Brigid. We need to plan our attack." Torrian locked gazes with his uncle before shifting his attention to the others.

Tormod could see the expressions on all of the men's faces change. It took great preparation to fight an enemy. They all stared at Logan Ramsay, awaiting his response to the Ramsay chieftain.

Logan clasped his hands behind his back. "Here's what I suggest. I'd like to wait until Jamie and the other guards arrive so we can better our odds. They should be here in another two days. They had orders to follow me if MacNiven was not seen in their path. We can attack near dusk on whatever day they return. I sent a message to my brother to send another two score of guards.

"If they have less than fifty guards, and I can get our number close to four score, we should be able to take them out easily with few losses on our part. Presumably, a message has already been sent to the king for ransom. For now, I'd like to send guards around the periphery to report on any other arrivals. I also plan to divide us up when we attack. I need to strategize on where to send my best archers and swordsmen."

He turned to Torrian. "Do you agree, my laird?"

Tormod knew he addressed his nephew this way for the benefit of the guards. He'd seen him address him much more informally before, but this was an unusual situation. There was no animosity or jealousy between them at all, and he hoped they would continue to work together this well.

Torrian showed no emotion in his response. "I do. I know your usual tactics, Uncle. Who have you chosen to go after the lasses? I know you usually send a team in to fetch the captives."

"I do. Molly will go. She is the fastest. I had planned to send Gwyneth with her, but I'll need to find another, and I think…"

"Not Sorcha," Torrian whispered. "She's not ready."

"I agree. Sorcha will serve us best in the trees as an archer. Her mother can be nearby. I need to find another to send in with Molly, so I wish to watch the guards practice their skills before I make my choice, which is one of the reasons we've separated from the women. I'd appreciate your input, Chief."

Tormod's stomach dropped to his toes. Molly? He was sending Molly into the worst of the battle?

Hellfire. Tormod had work to do if he was to prove himself to Logan Ramsay. He would not be able to handle it if another lad was sent in with her.

Something hit him that he hadn't expected. Molly meant more to him than just a pretty lass who'd caught his eye or a warrior whose skills and intelligence he respected.

He was falling hard for Molly Ramsay.

◆————◇————◆

Molly and Sorcha sat on either side of their mother on the log.

"Mama, does it hurt much?" Molly asked.

"As long as I do not move it or stand on it." Every so often she took several deep breaths, which indicated to Molly she was deeply in pain. But she knew her mother, she would never let on—if she did, Logan would keep her out of the battle completely. Her mother would not accept that.

"Oh, Mama," Molly leaned her head against her mother's shoulder. "I'm so sorry. What will we do without you running with us? You'll have to stay on horseback."

"You'll do what you need to in order to save your sister and your cousin. It angers me that this fool and his friends have spent so much time stealing our clan away, but 'tis the way of men these days, apparently. Lily, Aline, Heather, and now the wee ones."

"But you cannot run with Da. Who will go with him?" Sorcha whispered as she hugged her mother tight. "You always go with Da."

"Da's not going this time."

A chorus of "What?" erupted from both sisters.

"What do you mean Da is not going? He has to save Brigid and Jennet." Sorcha's eyes filled with tears.

"Listen. Your father and I are getting older, if you have not noticed. Just as Uncle Quade and Uncle Alex..."

"Uncle Alex? What's wrong with Uncle Alex?" Molly could not believe what her mother was suggesting about her dearest family members and their occasional failings. True, Uncle Quade had trouble with his knee and traveled on horseback as much as he could, and she was aware Uncle Alex had a wee problem with soreness in his joints. He was still as strong a warrior as ever, though, as was her sire.

Or were they?

"Uncle Alex is fine. He does a commendable job hiding his aches and pains, but I know his joints are bothering him. Your mother and father are slowing, too. We used to be the fastest, but that's no longer the case. I believe you may recall who usually wins the races we hold in the fields." She gave Molly a pointed look.

"Me?" Molly yelped. Her hand flew up to her throat as she bolted upright, letting go of her mother. "True, I win races, but Sorcha is always right behind me." She could not slow her racing heartbeat no matter how she tried.

"Nay, not right behind you. You are always way ahead of me," Sorcha stammered.

"But you beat the lads..."

"Aye, but I'm too young to go...am I not, Mama?" Sorcha's eyes had grown into orbs the size of the moon, terror laced through them.

Her mother patted her hand. "Calm down, both of you. We would not send you into aught you are not ready for. Sorcha, you will stay near me and shoot from a tree. Molly, I cannot run after your sister. As I'm sure your sire is telling the other guards, we've decided to send you after the girls."

"Alone?" Her voice came out in a squeak.

"Nay. Your father and Torrian will decide who will assist and protect you. You've been well-trained for this."

"But I always thought I would go with you, Mama, not without you." She fought the tears that threatened to drench her face. This was the opportunity she'd always hoped for, but she'd envisioned it differently.

"I know, but this was not planned, and Jennet and Brigid's lives are at stake. We need you."

Molly rested her elbows on her knees and gripped the sides of her head as she slumped down on the log. "When?"

"While we wait for Jamie and the others to arrive, your father and Torrian will test the skills of the warriors we have with us to decide who will go with you—and what exactly the others will be doing."

Molly got up from the log and headed off into the trees, moving as if in a trance.

"Molly?" her mother's voice followed her.

She angled her head just a notch to answer her mother. "Mama, I need a moment."

As soon as she put a little distance between herself and the group, she found herself standing and staring up into the treetops above her, watching the bare branches sway slightly in the breeze. She removed one of her gloves to tie up some strands of hair that had escaped their binding. A sound came from behind her, and she spun around in fear.

Her gaze stared straight into Tormod's chest. He reached for her bare hand. "Lass, you should keep it covered. 'Tis like ice." He wrapped his large hands around her chilled one and brought it up to his mouth, close enough for his breath to heat her palm.

That spare contact sent a surge of warmth through her. She lifted her eyes to his face, letting herself take comfort from the sight of him.

"You're trembling. Why?"

"They're sending me into the castle after Jennet and Brigid."

"Your sire told us. He also said he would send one of us as your protector. Trust me that I am doing all I can to be that person. I swear on my life to keep you safe." He ran the back of his fingers down her cheek. "You believe in yourself, do you not?"

She leaned into him and rested her cheek on his chest, reveling in the strong, steady beat of his heart against her ear. "Aye, but I do not wish to go alone. I would feel better if you were by my side."

His hand found its way to the nape of her neck, caressing her just at the base of her hairline, something that was so incredibly soothing it made her moan out loud.

His breath warmed her ear, her skin, even her soul. Not willing to lift her head away from his heat, she whispered, "Fight for me. I wish it to be you and no one else."

His hand slid around to cup her cheek, lifting her lips to his. He kissed her and she melted into him, their tongues dueling, igniting the desire for more, but he ended the kiss with a sigh and planted a light peck on her forehead. "If I wish to win the right to travel with you, I must go."

She could hear her sire prompting to the other guards. Aye, as much as she wished to stand here with him forever, she knew he had to leave. With a heavy heart, she stepped away from him. "Go and make my sire proud. Please." He took off toward the other guards, but not without a backward glance and a small grin intended just for her.

When he disappeared from her line of sight, she pivoted to return to her mother. Gwyneth didn't say anything to her, she just patted the log next to her, and when Molly sat, she took her hand—silently giving her comfort.

Sorcha hurried over to sit on Molly's other side. "You can do it, Mol. You always were the fastest and the best archer. You have to do it. You're our best chance."

Molly glanced first at her mother and then her sister and then nodded. Aye, she could probably do it.

Now she just had to convince herself of that truth and pray that Tormod would be by her side.

CHAPTER SIXTEEN

R ANULF MACNIVEN STOOD ATOP HIS curtain wall near the front
gates. His guards had thought they'd seen something, but they'd
come up dry. He'd sent off his two messages, one to King Alexander and
the other one requesting assistance from an old friend. It had been two
days since the messages had been sent. Something should be happening
at this point.

As if the beasts from the underworld had heard him, he saw a movement across his land. He squinted, hoping someone had come with a
response to one of his messages.

Walrick and Earc came to stand beside him. A wide grinned crossed
his face as the visitor came closer.

"Who is it?" Walrick asked. "Must I get my arrow out?"

"Nay. 'Tis a beautiful woman. Please do not put an arrow through her
heart. I need her desperately." The memory of her voluptuous curves in
his hands made him hard, so he spun around and walked away from his
men, climbing down from the wall. Before he left, he bellowed to his
guards at the gate, "Let her and her escorts in when she arrives. I need
all the men I can get in case those foolish Ramsays decide to attack. Of
course, if they do, I'll kill those lassies instantly. We shall see."

Davina of Buchan. How long had it been since he'd set eyes upon her?
He'd watched her from afar for a while after his close escape from the
hangman's noose, but then he'd had to run for fear of discovery. How
he'd missed her. He'd feared she had married while he was away and
would not come, but love conquered all. He whistled as he moved into

the great hall and his chamber above stairs, doing his best to make himself presentable. She'd always been fastidious about his cleanliness, so he changed his tunic, washed his hands and face, cleaned his teeth with a cloth, and then chewed on mint leaves when he finished.

He hoped he could convince Davina to watch over the girls in his solar. Cedrica and Lorna refused to go inside with the lassies, too afraid of curses and critters. They were also getting anxious, asking too many questions. He wanted someone in the chamber with the wee ones, someone who could command their respect and control, someone who could kill them if necessary. He could not count on his men to do it after the wee episode with Bearchun in the courtyard. Witch or not, the one called Jennet made him queasy as well. Bearchun had been so undone, he'd run off as soon as he'd come to, taking Shaw with him.

Davina would do anything he asked of her, especially once he promised marriage to her. He would promise her whatever she wanted so long as she helped him in this final endeavor. Besides, he could not wait to climb between her sweet thighs once he was declared free and chieftain of his own land again. They were fabulous in bed together.

He whistled again as he moved down the stairs to the great hall, almost making it to the door before it swung open.

There she stood, a vision of dark beauty adorned in deep blue. She froze in place as soon as her gaze caught his.

Ranulf held his arms open to her. "Come to me, my sweet. How I've missed you."

Davina, still frozen in her spot, only moved when the guard behind her ushered her inside and closed the door against the cold winter blast. She looked transfixed, almost as if she'd seen a ghost. In a way, she had.

"Chief, do you have an ale for our parched throats?" the guard asked and stepped around her, opening the door for his comrades to join him.

MacNiven nodded his head and tipped it toward the great hall. "My servants will take care of you." The eight guards who'd come with her hurried over to a table, leaving Davina alone with him. He took a step closer. "Did you miss me, my love?"

Davina stared at her gloved hands, tears sliding down her cheeks. "I had no idea where you were. I tried to visit you before...before the hanging...I tried, but you were not there. I saw a different man in your cell."

"Och, amazing what a wee bit of coin can do. The man would have died within a few moons. I paid him enough coin for his wife to keep their home and buy food for his two bairns. He was happy to take my place. 'Tis less painful to die quickly than slowly over three or four moons."

"What happened to you? Why have you not come to me before this? I loved you."

He tugged her over near the hearth. "I could not. I had to stay away until the search for me slowed. I was deep in the Highlands."

"What about now? Are they not searching for you still?" She gave him the demurest look he'd ever seen from her. His gaze narrowed as he assessed the woman he'd had such strong feelings for a long time ago. He couldn't say it was love. Alas, could he ever love a woman? Probably not. Now he loved power more, but she could still prove beneficial to him and his pursuits.

He grazed her lips with his finger and then lifted her chin to him and devoured her with his mouth, teasing her with his tongue until she fell under his spell, moaning and wrapping her arms around his neck.

"I still love you, Ranulf."

He pulled back and kissed her nose. "Good. I wish I could take you to my chamber and spend the day with you, but there are pressing matters that require my attention. I have kidnapped two wee Ramsay lassies and I wish for you to watch over them."

"Nay, Ranulf." She stepped away from him, as if she needed to allow this new development to settle. He supposed it was a surprise.

"Not the Ramsays." Her hand covered her mouth as she backed away from him. "Why must you go after the Ramsays? Can you not buy your freedom? Why must all the men I know steal women? 'Tis wrong… so wrong. If you bought your freedom on a ship, we could run away together, live a wonderful life with bairns and…"

He scowled, not willing to change his plans. He'd thought this through very carefully. "Nay, I'm tired of running. I have planned this wisely. Their lives for mine. King Alexander will give me my freedom in exchange for the safe return of the lasses. We just have to wait a bit longer, and then we can live wherever we choose. You'll see." There was no need for her to know he'd kill the lasses if necessary. Davina was too soft-hearted to know his true plans.

Of course, he still needed to make a decision as to what his final plans were. He stared over her shoulder at the huge sword on the wall, his sire's. For his sire, he knew he should do all in his power to gain his land and title back. The only way that could happen was if he returned the lassies and the king granted him his freedom. Then he could live here, marry Davina, and have Walrick as his second.

But Walrick would never stay. He was hungry for coin and distant lands. The thought of leaving Scotland enticed Ranulf. *That* would be true freedom. Thanks to Hew Gordon, he still had plenty of coin, so it was possible.

Or mayhap he should purchase his own ship and crew to sail the seas. Or…

"Ranulf? Are you listening to me?" Davina's unwavering dark gaze settled on him.

"Of course, love," he replied. Of course, his declarations of love were naught but bold lies—he'd never felt that emotion, not for anyone, but he did what he needed to do. Always had.

"Then why did you want me here now?" She tossed her mantle off to the side and began to pace in an odd pattern.

This was not the same woman he'd once known. Davina of Buchan had been strong and independent before the fiasco in Edinburgh. Those were the characteristics that had drawn him to her—bold, brazen, strong, and confident. This woman was riddled with doubts, and she clearly didn't trust him.

Shite, but he had to keep her on his side. He could not lose her now. What had happened to her since the fiasco at the Ramsays? "Because I need your help. I want you to watch the lassies. The one claims to be a witch and has managed to frighten many of my guards away. Don't you see, Davina? Once the exchange is made, you and I can marry and live here together—me as chief of my castle, and you as my wife. What more could you want? I'll dress you in the finest gowns and buy you the most beautiful gemstones in all the land."

She kneaded her hands together, but then lifted her gaze to his. "All right. I'll agree to watch the lassies, but only if you promise never to leave me again."

"Once I have my freedom, I will defer to you in all my plans for the future. Is that fair enough for you?"

The first smile he'd seen crossed her face. "Aye, 'tis fair."

Ranulf headed to his solar, beckoning for Davina to follow him. Once there, he turned around to face her. "I'm grateful to you for doing this for me."

"Who are the two women by the door?" Davina asked. "Why are they not inside with the lassies?"

He pulled her close enough to cup her bottom, caressing the full globe as she wriggled in his hand. "They are out here because they cannot manage two wee lassies. Can you imagine such a thing? Now, I know you are more than capable."

"Of course, I am." She sighed, glaring at the two women seated on the floor. "I'll do it. But remember all you've promised me."

He opened the door, Davina stepped inside, and he closed the door behind her.

As soon as he did, Cedrica and Lorna bounced to their feet. "Which is it? Are you running south with Walrick and taking us along, or are you staying here? Please say you do not plan to kill the lassies, that you will indeed return them to the Ramsays. Are they not leverage for you to get what you want? We'll not kill them. We want no part of that, Dubh. They'll punish us right along with you."

"This time, I'll not get caught—I'll be freed instead." And his mind burst with joy at the thought. He'd be the best in all the land. Soon the King of the Scots would do his bidding. He just couldn't decide what to do. Should he go to England, or buy a galley ship? He could buy the oarsmen to go along with them. His smile widened at the thought of being the captain at the helm of his ship.

Or should he stay here with sweet Davina? He had so many choices.

"Unless you kill the lassies," Cedrica barked. "If you kill two wee lasses, they'll hang you, especially Ramsay lasses."

"Keep your voice down. They are just inside." Dubh glowered at Cedrica. Now they were being difficult. Fine. He'd find someone to tie them up to ensure they made no trouble. As soon as he could, he'd send them to Edinburgh and get his coin for them. "I'm not asking you to kill them. I'll take care of it." He waved them over to the guards eating at the trestle table. "Find yourselves something to eat."

The two rushed over to the table. When he passed by his guards to head out the door, he leaned down and whispered to one of them, "Tie those two up and leave them in the corner."

Good. All was in place as planned. They just had to await the king's response.

◆———○———◆

Tormod swung his sword over his head, bringing it down on Kyle Maule's weapon as hard as he could. To his surprise, Torrian's second dropped to one knee as he blocked the blow, though he recovered nicely.

"Well done, Moriston," Logan shouted loud enough for all to hear. "Though Maule, the poor lad, has an excuse. The bairn has kept him up at night, so he's not well rested."

Kyle glared at Logan. "The babe has not been born yet. But it is due any day, and Lily is verra uncomfortable. Do not worry about me. I am strong as ever."

The distant sound of horses brought their swordplay to a halt. They'd moved farther away from the MacNiven castle to keep from being discovered. Tormod hoped their reinforcements had arrived. Logan and Torrian wished to attack as soon as possible.

Torrian hurried over to get a look at the riders, and his face lit up with recognition. "Jamie. That was a quick journey for them. We did not expect his team for another half day."

As the guards dismounted, Logan slung up onto his horse and rode over to the group—they needed to be warned to keep the extra guards well back from the area.

Once Jamie reached the group in the small clearing, Torrian asked, "Any problems?"

Jamie was followed by Gregor, Gavin, Braden, and Coll. The other guards had stayed back to take care of the horses.

"I have to wonder myself why you have returned so quickly." Logan said. "Is there trouble?"

Jamie held his hands up, palm out, in a calming gesture. "First, answer me this. Have you located MacNiven?"

"Aye, he's inside his curtain wall with some of his loyal followers," Torrian said. "We think Jennet and Brigid are there, though no one has seen them. What did you learn from the king?"

"We never made it to the king. We intercepted a messenger from a Chief Dubh, as he's calling himself. He wants his freedom and the return of his land in exchange for the lassies."

"Did you send the messenger on to the king?"

"Aye. Braden convinced him to reveal all to us first."

Logan raised a brow but said nothing. "Then I predict that the king will be here soon."

"Why would the king come himself?" Torrian asked. "Why not just send his warriors to assist us?"

That earned a bellowed laugh. "Our king is in such a fury over Ranulf MacNiven that his stable boy will be saddling his horse the very instant after the messenger delivers his tidings. He will be here, though I cannot predict when, or what he will choose to do once he arrives." Logan began to pace, something he did not see him do often. It was a rare sign of nerves in the great man.

"MacNiven also demanded the king be here in his message. Based on our location when we met with the messenger, the king should arrive on the morrow," Jamie said. "Do you have a plan in place?"

"I'll get Gwyneth and the girls to join us," Torrian said.

Once they were all together, including a few of the guards who'd hung back, Logan and Torrian revealed their plan.

"I'll give specific assignments in a moment," Logan said, "but we'll attack in three different ways. First, we'll ram through the gate and attack on horseback and on foot. I've watched many of you work, and I'm impressed. We should have no problem overtaking them with our swords. We'll also have a group of archers in the trees. And Molly will be going in after the lassies while I stay back with Gwyneth. Without knowing for certain when the king and his guards will arrive, we cannot wait for them before we attack."

"Molly is the fastest," Jamie said, "but are you sending her in alone?"

"Nay, Tormod goes with her."

Tormod had to hide his reaction to Logan's announcement. Nothing could have pleased him more. He needed to be with Molly, protect her from any harm. It would not do to have anyone there but him.

Logan continued. "I've observed his skills over the past days, and I believe he's the best equipped to switch from sword to bow with ease if necessary. Eat and prepare yourselves. We go in at dusk, and we will not stop until we have Jennet and Brigid back."

Pleased that Logan recognized that fact, he did his best to control his urge to shout to the heavens above that his hard work had been rewarded. Tormod could feel the excitement build among his peers. He knew what it was like to head into battle, how you had to depend on everyone to back you up. He glanced at Molly to see how she had handled the news, but he could not tell.

Logan gestured to him. "We'd like to speak to the two of you."

Tormod walked behind Molly, her gaze on the ground as she did as she was instructed. "My thanks for your faith in my skills, my lord," Tormod said to Logan.

"Well deserved, Moriston. Now protect my daughter. Here is what we think will happen."

Once they settled on the log around her mother, her sire brought oatcakes for each of them along with a skin of water.

Gwyneth addressed them first. "The guards will ram the gate down, and your job is to run to the periphery as soon as they take the courtyard. You should be able to run around them. Molly, Tormod will lead with his sword in hand, and you can use your bow as you see fit. But your job is not to stay and battle but to move into the keep, searching all the chambers for the lassies. Once you find them, hide them in a safe place until we are in control of the situation. Do not try to came back out into the melee with the two wee ones, 'tis too dangerous."

"And what if we do not find them?"

Gwyneth sighed. "I hope it does not come to that, but if it does, question whomever you discover: kitchen help, stable lads, everyone. If there's a back entrance, MacNiven might try to run with the lassies. Look around and follow where you must. You will be able to run faster because the lassies will slow his movement."

Tormod glanced at Logan. "What weapon do you expect MacNiven to use if he's on the run?"

"Anything he can," Logan replied. "I suspect he'll have a couple of archers as protection. Word is he's got one of the best archers, though of course that cannot be true since all of the best archers are in our clan or the Grants. Ashlyn Grant has built herself a reputation since she wounded the man." Logan added, "But cunning is his best weapon. That's what has gotten him this far. Be thinking."

"And run like the fastest deer you've ever seen," Gwyneth whispered. "They'll never be able to hit you, daughter."

CHAPTER SEVENTEEN

DAVINA STARED AT THE TWO girls huddled on the floor in the corner, one almost behind the other. Jennet, the one who had ruined her life, locked gazes with her. She clearly had no fear.

"Look who we have here," Davina drawled. "The wee lassie who ruined my life. I finally have you in my clutches." She clenched both her hands into fists as she snarled at the two girls.

"I know not of what you speak. How could a wee lassie ruin your life? You are responsible for whatever you do, not me." Jennet swung her plait behind her head.

The little one next to her nodded vehemently. "My mama says the same all the time. Be 'sponsible." She rested her head on the other girl's shoulder, their hands entwined.

"Jennet is your name, if I recall correctly. What is your name?" She pointed to the one she didn't recognize as she sauntered closer to them.

"Her name is Brigid, and you will not intimidate me," Jennet declared with a bounce of her head.

Brigid lifted her head to mimic Jennet's head bounce perfectly, though her gaze was on the floor. "You will not inta...ina...scare me either."

"I do not need to scare you, you are my prisoner, so you can do naught."

"If you had a heart, you would help us escape," Jennet announced.

Davina chuckled. "If I had a heart...hmmm..."

Brigid perked up, her eyes wide. "Do you not have one? A heart?"

Jennet gave her cousin a disparaging look. "Of course she has a heart, or she would not be alive and talking."

Brigid scowled and stared at her hands. "Mayhap she does, but she does not use it overmuch. She's mean, just like he is."

"I'm mean? Is that what you said?" Davina crossed her arms and tossed her head back with a laugh, circling the room to appear like a vulture, anything to gain their fear.

Brigid shrugged her shoulders. "I want my mama." She rubbed one eye with her knuckle.

"I tire of you two already. Brigid—" she pointed to the opposite corner, "—you are to sit over there. I do not like the two of you together."

Brigid grabbed onto her cousin, tears welling in her eyes. "Nay, please allow me to stay here. I'll not say another word."

Davina jumped toward them, delivering her command with a roar. "Now!" Why did the two wee things bother her so? And why had Ranulf insisted she watch the girls when there were two able bodies outside the door? Actually, now that she thought about it, what was the purpose of those two sitting on their arses? She hated this assignment, and she had questions for Ranulf.

Jennet jumped up and scampered to the other corner. "I'll go, Brigie." She plopped into the corner with a huff. "My mama would not like you. You are not verra considerate of others."

"Not 'siderate at all." Tears slid down Brigid's cheeks.

Shite, she hated it when girls cried. Had no one ever taught them not to cry as her sire had taught her? It had taken an inner strength she hadn't known she possessed, but she had learned—the hard way. "Just be quiet."

Jennet stared at her cousin in the corner. "Do you not recall having a friend or a sister or a cousin when you were small? We prefer to be together."

"Nay, I had no lasses in my family, and I was not allowed to play with the servants' bairns. I did just fine on my own." However, she recalled a few lonely nights when she'd cried herself to sleep wishing for a friend. Nay, she did fine on her own, just as she'd said.

"It would seem not," Jennet mumbled as she played with the folds in her skirt.

"What did you say, you wee bitch?" Davina crept toward her in a crouched position.

"Naught, I said naught that needs to be repeated. I'll be quiet."

Davina grabbed the front of the lassie's gown, lifting her off the floor.

"What did you mean by that?" How she wished she did not care what others thought, but alas, she did. She was obsessed with what others thought of her—her true failing, Ranulf called it.

"It means I wish you had experienced friendship. It means I love my cousin, and I'm sorry you do not have the same in your life."

Davina dropped her back to the ground. "I do not need a friend."

"Mayhap not, but you would be happier if you had one. Brigie understands me. When our mamas do not understand us, we talk to each other. We both know what 'tis like to be the youngest in the family." Jennet straightened her skirts underneath her.

Brigid said, "Aye, I love my cousin more than any. My brothers are idiots sometimes, but not Jennet."

"Ranulf understands me," Davina said. "He's all I need. I do not need cousins or sisters."

"Why? He cannot be verra nice to you. 'Tis not in his nature."

"Ranulf loves me."

"But why do you love him? He'll not be with you when this is over." Jennet stared up at the beams in the ceiling.

"Aye, he will. He promised me that we will marry and live together wherever I'd like. Mind your tongue, lass." More bothered than she cared to let on, she paced in a circle. Ranulf loved her still, did he not? Had he not been excited to see her? She stopped short before continuing to pace. He wasn't the same as he had been before all this had happened. She couldn't be sure what had changed about him, but there was something... She chewed on her one worn fingernail, the one she chewed most. "Why do you say that? Where do you think he will be when this is over?"

Jennet shrugged one shoulder, glancing around the chamber and then at the door. Her voice came out in a whisper, "Because I heard him tell one man that they were leaving for England after this."

Davina's eyes widened before she spun on her heel to head toward the door. She opened it and bellowed into the great hall. "Ranulf!"

◆━━━◇━━━◆

Molly's heart pounded so hard, she thought it would burst through her skin. Her mother hopped up on one leg to speak to her. "Now listen, love, you can do this. I believe in you, and so does your father. Do you believe you can do this?"

She thought for a moment, and then nodded. It was true. After much inner turmoil, she could now say she was ready. Tormod stood a few steps behind her while her mother went over her instructions. She wished to tell him how much it meant to have him standing behind her, a tower of strength that would get her through this. With his support, she was actually beginning to believe she could do this and make her parents proud. She hoped to see her sister's smiling face again soon.

"They will start ramming the gates with the logs in a few moments, once darkness settles. You must be ready and alert at all times. God speed, and Tormod, watch over her."

Her mother kissed both her cheeks and then let Logan lift her up onto her horse.

"Mama, stay safe. Be careful. And Sorcha, stay in the trees." Her sister waved to her as they moved off to the spot they'd chosen.

Her sire leaned over and kissed her on the cheek. "We will get the bastard, Molly, and you'll find our lassies. I've always known you had it in you. He's no better than Randall Baines."

How had her sire known that name would give her the push she needed? Baines was the son of the Englishwoman she'd served for a short time, and oh, how she hated him.

Her family left her side and she turned to see her brother and cousins bringing one log forward as quietly as possible, and the guards bringing another. She and Tormod stood a ways back from the curtain wall. The logs were almost close enough to be seen, but they'd waited until dark in order to hide their movements as much as possible. They would attack on Torrian's instructions.

She took a deep breath and pursed her lips, letting her breath out slowly, trying to slow her racing heart.

Tormod reached over and squeezed her hand. "We can do this. Your sire and cousins will take down that bastard, and we'll find your sister and cousin. All will be over by morn." The sun had just set, and some of MacNiven's guards could be heard deep in their cups, just as her sire had predicted.

"I know, but I always thought that if I ever had something important to do, a rescue or aught like it, I'd be with my mama, and her guidance would carry me through it. I'd hoped word would travel as far as England, and my true sire would hear about how my mother and I had battled evil and won. That chance is gone forever."

"Will I not serve as a suitable substitute? While I'm not the archer your mother is, I will fight for you. Together, we shall find the lassies and get them back where they belong. I look forward to working through this together. I'm honored and proud of both of us. Give *us* a chance."

Tormod had managed to give everything a completely different slant. What if another lad had been chosen? The thought almost sickened her. They were together—that mattered. She needed to look at things differently. Leaning against him, she rested her head on his shoulder. "Aye, I am so grateful you will be by my side. Do not misunderstand me, but 'tis as if my insides have turned into a basketful of frogs. My mother calms me. You excite me, something entirely different."

That earned her a wee smile. "Do not doubt your mother," he said. "She'll soon be back to spying along with your sire. Look at this as your chance to make her proud."

She pivoted to face him. How she wished she could run her fingers through his hair and kiss him right then and there. "Tormod, you draw out what is best in me. It does not matter if anyone knows 'tis us. What matters most is saving my sister and my cousin, and getting rid of scum like MacNiven. 'Tis what our king wants. I'm sure of it."

"Tell me about your sister, Brigid. No one talks about her, and I fear bringing up her name."

She smiled as soon as he said her sister's name. How she loved Brigid. "Brigid makes everyone smile. She has the biggest heart of all of us. One of Jennet and Brigid's favorite things to do is to save animals. They are quite entertaining because they rescue animals so often. A moon ago, Brigid found a newborn animal left to die underneath a tree. She brought it to Aunt Brenna, and they determined it was a red squirrel. Aunt Brenna gave them the tools they would need to raise the squirrel to adulthood, and they did. It's wonderful how they work together. Jennet is the healer, and she determines the correct way for them to treat their patients, how often, what to feed them, and so on. Brigid is the nurturer. Thinking of how she held that baby squirrel in her wee hands makes me almost cry. She would sing to him, pet him, and cuddle him all day. My mother had to tell her no squirrels in their bed at night."

"Did he survive?"

"Aye. He's still their pet. He plays with them equally, just as if they were his mama and papa."

Torrian's voice ripped out the Ramsay war whoop, which his guards immediately joined.

The first log hit the gates and chaos erupted. Molly squeezed Tormod's hand, waiting for their instructions to move.

There was no turning back now.

CHAPTER EIGHTEEN

CHIEF DUBH STOOD ON THE steps to his great hall, wondering why the foreboding feeling that had descended upon him wouldn't leave. He pivoted on his heel and headed back into the hall, just in time to see Davina run out of the solar, her destination clear as she made her way toward him.

"What is it? You are supposed to be watching over my treasures." One hand rubbed his chin as he did his best to give Davina his attention. He'd given her such simple instructions, but she could not follow them. How difficult could two lassies be?

He headed toward the door but then whirled around and headed toward the kitchen, then changing his mind and heading toward Davina. "What is it? Can you not see how busy I am?"

"Ranulf, the girls told me you were planning to go to the south of England. Are you leaving the land of the Scots, or are you staying here? You said we could go wherever I pleased after we marry. I do not wish to be so far away from my sire. I'm all he has left."

He did his best not to roll his eyes. God's teeth, but what did she want from him? He might stay, he might leave for England, or he might even sail on the high seas.

"Ranulf? Do you love me or not?"

The desire to reach out to wring her pretty little neck was almost irrepressible, but he decided at the last minute that this was not a good time. "Of course, I love you. We'll do whatever pleases you. Now go back inside and guard my treasures."

A loud banging ripped through the air, followed by another and another and another.

"What the hell?" He flew to the door, yanking it open to stare out at his curtain wall. Men raced about his keep, collecting swords and bows as they went. "What is it?"

Earc ran to his side. "They're ramming the gates."

"Get your arse over there and fight, you fool!" Ranulf's hand flew to his forehead after he shoved Earc away from him. "Halt, Earc."

Earc spun around, a wild look on his face. "What is it?"

"Who? Who are the men outside the gates?"

"They're in Ramsay plaids and Grant plaids, Chief." He waited for directions.

"Bastards! Send Ninean to me."

"But he's going up the wall to shoot at the invaders."

"I do not care what he is doing. You have your orders. Send Ninean to me. Now go." Ninean was his best archer. He needed his protection for himself and guards for the girls.

Earc took off toward the gates as the ramming continued, so loud he thought his ears would burst open. Ranulf opened the door and ran back into the great hall. "Davina!"

She popped out of the solar. "What is it? And what is that blasted noise, Ranulf?"

"We're under attack. The savages are back."

He twirled around and strode back toward the door, bellowing over his shoulder, "Get the lasses and wait in the hall for me. We're leaving. I have planned out a strategy. This is no surprise. I will win this."

He stomped down the stairs and into his courtyard, pounding his chest. "I will win this time and reign supreme!"

"You'll all be dead, Ramsays, along with your wee ones. Dead!"

Tormod glanced over at Molly. "Are you ready? The gates are about to fall." He could see how her anticipation was getting the best of her, from her wide eyes to the tic of her jaw to the softness of her gaze when she looked at him. "Believe that we'll do this together."

She looked almost ready to bolt when a voice yelled to them. "Molly, not until I give you clearance." Jamie was on horseback, waiting directly behind the warriors who were hefting the giant log. "We go ahead of you."

Moments later, the gate collapsed and the lads dropped the log, both events resulting in a deafening crash. Horse hooves pounded as their full force of around seventy guards rushed into the curtain wall. Arrows flew from overhead, taking out many of the first MacNiven guards to fly through the gate.

Comrades carrying torches moved inside to set fire to anything that would burn. Jamie finally waved to him and Molly from his horse. "Run behind me and off to the side. I'll cover you."

Torrian was leading guards on the opposite side of Jamie. This was it. Tormod grabbed Molly's hand to keep her protected behind him. "Come and ready your bow." He unsheathed his sword, ready to take out anyone who came near his Molly. All of a sudden, everything seemed so clear. It felt like they belonged together, side by side. And despite his readiness to fight for his love, for those two innocent girls, he felt calm, confident. With Molly, *for* her, he could do anything.

The battle was here.

◆─────○─────◆

Ranulf MacNiven shoved the door open with his shoulder, allowing himself the chance to glance back at the chaos in his courtyard. The rotten savages were intent on ruining all his plans.

Again.

But not this time. He was no longer Ranulf MacNiven, but Chief Dubh—and Dubh had anticipated exactly what was unfolding in front of him. Ninean rushed up to him, his bow in his hand. "Aye, Dubh?"

"You and Walrick shall both go with me. Your job is to protect me. This attack is no surprise. I knew it would take place at night. 'Tis why I've planned around it. All we need is Walrick, and we are ready to leave."

Ninean nodded and followed him into the great hall. Davina, looking as gorgeous as ever, stood in the middle of the hall, one hand on each of the lassies, though they fought like wee creatures from the dead.

"Enough!" he bellowed to the two of them. He charged across the hall and raised his hand to swing at one of them, but Davina raised both of her hands to stop him.

"Ranulf, they're bairns. Leave them be. 'Tis frightening enough for them. You've stolen them and starved them."

He dropped his arm and growled at her through clenched teeth. "Do not ever do that again. Now, grab them both and get ready. We are leaving as soon as Walrick arrives."

Spinning on his heel, he moved to the door, peeking out for a moment.

"Where are you taking us? Ranulf, they'll kill us if we try to leave now." Davina followed him and yanked on his tunic. "Leave the lassies and run away with me."

"Nay." He whirled around to face her. "I am done running. 'Tis all the Ramsays' fault...all of it. Every misfortune that has been dealt me is because of the Ramsays. They'll pay."

Walrick stepped inside. "Dubh. What next? They've killed more than half our men."

"Come, Davina. We're going out through the door in the curtain wall and heading for a deserted hut straight west. We'll hide there, and my archer will kill them all before they can find their way inside."

Walrick's face lit up. "Then 'tis time for us to take our leave. They can have your keep."

"There...there are quite a few of them," Ninean stammered. "They outnumber us by far. If they come for us..."

"We'll kill them. I have their wee lassies. No one will dare attack us in the cottage, or I'll kill their dear girls. Mayhap I'll deliver one head to convince them."

Brigid screamed, and Davina reached for MacNiven, shoving against his chest with all the power she had. "Nay. I'll not allow it. Kill any man you wish, but you'll not be hurting these innocent bairns."

He struggled with his footing at first, but then planted his feet wide and grabbed her by both arms, lifting her into the air. "Then you'll stay here. Walrick, grab one of the lassies and I'll take the other. I needed your loyalty, Davina, but you are only loyal to your sire. I'll not travel with anyone who cannot demonstrate their loyalty to me. Be gone, I wish never to see you again."

Davina fled into the solar and slammed the door behind her.

Chief Dubh picked up Brigid and headed to the kitchens in the back of the building. Walrick followed with a snort, grabbing Jennet on the way. She hit him once and Walrick put his face close to hers. "Do it again, if you will, because I hit back. See how many swats you can take, lass, from this hand."

Dubh couldn't help but chuckle at the look on the lass's face when she saw the size of the hand Walrick held up.

Jennet kept her hands to herself as the five of them headed into the kitchens. "Ninean, you shall run behind us and shoot anyone you see.

Once we get inside the hut and the lassies are hidden, we'll do our negotiating. When we arrive, find good trees to hide in."

They were about to step outside when he came upon Cedrica and Lorna, each tied up and squirming on the floor. He called out to one of his men outside. "Put these two in the solar, and leave them tied up."

Dubh smiled as soon as they stepped out of the kitchens. "You see? Just as I expected. No one is behind the wall. Off we go!" They raced off into the dark, leaving the others behind in the hall.

Jennet looked at Brigid from underneath the big arm that held her tight to the brute's side. Dubh wondered what the hell the lass was doing when she held her fingers up to her friend.

First one...

Then two...

Then three...

And the loudest screams he'd ever heard erupted from the two lassies.

◆————○————◆

Molly and Tormod raced into the thick of the skirmish, crouching off to the side and making sure they kept away from the densest part of the battle. The din of clashing metal, pained screams, and war whoops filled the air as they crept closer to the keep. They had almost reached the steps when Tormod caught sight of something through the haze of smoke. "There. A side door."

He led Molly in that direction, only stopping to take out one warrior as they hurried along. The sound of two arrows from Molly's bow buzzed by his ear, followed by a resounding yelp when she managed to hit her targets. He cracked the door open and peered inside to see if anyone was there, but the path was clear, so he ushered her in ahead of him. Once his eyes adjusted to the darkness, he saw a staircase sweeping up in one direction, and a door in the other. He pointed up the stairs.

"We'll search above stairs first." He led the way, surprised by how empty the hall appeared to be. Once they reached the passageway, lit by only a few torches, they moved from chamber to chamber, discouraged to find them all empty.

"Nay," Molly cried. "Brigid! Jennet? Where are you?"

The keep was surprisingly quiet. It was possible they'd been taken away somewhere, but they could not entertain that possibility until they'd checked the entire keep. "We'll look downstairs. They must be here somewhere." Tormod pointed to a spot where she could wait. "I must check first to see who's in the great hall."

The hall was eerily deserted, though the screams and shouts filtered in from outside. Once he was certain it was safe, he beckoned Molly down the stairs.

Molly raced down to him and clutched his hand. "I hear something from over there."

He glanced at the door that had captured her attention. Based on the location, it was likely the solar. Though he did his best to listen, he could not hear anything. She tugged him over to the door, which she pushed open before he could get her behind him. He quickly moved in front of her. Still, she stood on her tiptoes to peek over his shoulder.

There, in the middle of the solar, sat a woman prone on the floor, sobbing as if her world was about to end. Mayhap it was. Two other women sat tied up and gagged in the corner, both asleep. Had they been given something? Tormod stepped inside and held his sword out in front of him. "Where are the lassies?"

As the woman sat up and stared at him, he heard Molly gasp in recognition.

The woman just gave them a sad look and shook her head, staring at the floor.

CHAPTER NINETEEN

MOLLY GRIPPED TORMOD'S ARMS FROM behind as she stared at the woman. "Davina, where are the lassies?"

A sound interrupted all the noise from the battle, something so rare, so unusual among the shouts of a battle that it stood out loud and clear.

The screams of little girls.

"Tormod, that's Brigid. I'd know her scream anywhere." Molly was already out the door before she realized Tormod was not behind her.

Tormod was looking down at Davina with a hard look on his face. "Where? Where are they taking them?"

Davina was sobbing, but she managed to point toward the kitchens. "Out the back and west…to a hut. You need to save them. Ranulf said he would kill them, if necessary."

Without sparing another glance for her, Tormod turned and followed Molly out the door and to the kitchens. As soon as they stepped outside, they scanned the area and Tormod pointed west. "There, I think I see someone running."

Molly moaned as she sprinted in that direction. "They are too far ahead of us."

"We shall catch them. Have faith and run like a deer, just as your mother told you."

She nodded and took off, her eyes fixed on the one person she could see in the dark ahead of her, way ahead of her. She prayed for strength and ran and ran until she thought her chest would burst, finally turning around to see how Tormod was doing. Shocked to see how much he'd fallen behind, she waited for him to catch up.

"Tormod, can you not run faster? 'Tis the only chance we have to catch them."

Tormod came up behind her and stopped, bending over at the waist to catch his breath. "I cannot." He took three more deep breaths and whispered, "I cannot keep up with you. Go without me."

Molly shook her head in denial, but then in a shaky, halting voice, she whispered, "I cannot. I cannot do this alone. I need you with me."

He pushed off his legs and lumbered up to her, each gasp an effort for him, though she could hear her own short pants from her exertion. His hands cupped her face and he rested his forehead against hers. "Now, listen carefully to me, my love. You do not need me. You are the only chance we have at catching the bastards who took your sister and cousin. I will follow to back you up, but you have to run, run as though 'tis the only way you'll stop them."

A tear slid down her cheek and she whispered, "I do not want to go without...I cannot..."

His fingers fell to her lips and he said, "Hush. You will go. Make me proud, and do this on your own. I believe in you, and your sister needs you." He bent down to grab a clump of dirt and mud, rubbing it across her cheeks and forehead. "They'll not see you at all if I darken your face. Now go. Go, and you shall stop them. We're all counting on you."

He kissed her on the lips, and she nodded before she turned and ran off in the direction she'd seen the last person go. She picked up speed, telling herself she could do it, she just needed to run as fast as she could... just as she'd seen her mother do many times before. She'd make her mama and papa proud. And suddenly it was just as important for her to make Tormod proud.

She glanced over her shoulder once to see if she could see him. Though he was a good distance away from her, he was still running—just like he'd promised. "Go! Do not look back. I will be behind you. Run like God's beautiful creature that you are."

His belief in her made her legs churn faster and faster until she hit her prime, something that usually only happened when she was running alone, with no one else to watch her. She was free and quick, and she would find her dear sister and cousin before those lousy bastards hurt them.

Her eyes adjusted to the darkness and she dodged every obstacle, every tree branch, every hole in the ground, anything that would slow her.

She focused on the one spot in front of her that she thought was a man, and sure enough, the figure grew larger and larger as she kept running.

Sure of foot her father had called her often, and the boots her mother had made especially for her and all her siblings made no sound at all in the woods. As her feet carried her closer, the wind whistled by her ears—a sound that she loved—and eventually she could make out three figures ahead of her, all adults, and two of them were carrying moving bundles.

Brigid and Jennet. How she wished to yell out to the world that she was coming. Her gaze narrowed on her targets as she came closer, and she finally realized that they were slowing. A squat hut waited ahead. She hid behind a tree and watched them as she readied her bow, hoping to take at least one of the men out. The one man without a bundle under his arm climbed into a tree while the other two brought the girls into the hut. Once the man had settled in his perch, she took aim and fired, hitting him square in the chest. He fell to the ground, and she could tell from the angle that the fall had snapped his neck.

One down, two to go. She nocked another arrow, but the door opened and MacNiven came out, Brigid held in front of him. "Go ahead, shoot again and you'll kill Logan Ramsay's daughter."

She let her hand fall, watching him carefully, willing her sister to be strong. He spun about in a circle because he had no idea where she was hidden, and she mentally thanked Tormod for covering her face in dirt to help hide her in the dark.

She nocked her arrow and lined it up with him as he spun, but then he stopped, facing her. "Go ahead, shoot."

"Go ahead and turn around, and you have my promise that I will shoot. Give me your back again," she whispered to herself, never taking her eyes off the man. He still had no idea where she was.

But rather than turn around, he went back inside.

And then the worst thing possible happened.

A moment later, MacNiven emerged from the hut with Jennet in front of him, and another man followed him with Brigid in his arms. MacNiven said to him, "Go, Walrick. I'll take care of this situation. I'll meet you in our assigned place."

Walrick took off with Brigid and MacNiven stayed, finding a spot behind a large rock. He placed Jennet on top of the rock, her hands and feet tied, and held a dagger to her throat.

"Come out with your hands above your head or I'll cut her throat."

Which one did she choose—Brigid or Jennet?

◆————○————◆

Tormod watched Molly run off into the distance. Hellfire, but she was beautiful when she ran like that. He wished he could keep up with her, but only deer could run as she did.

He did something he rarely did as he chugged along behind her, following her path. He prayed. He prayed for two wee lassies, for the long-legged beauty in front of him, and for the chance to begin his life anew, away from his sire and his brother and his foolish sister-in-law. Now he recognized them for what they were—immature, childish, selfish. If he went back to Grant land, he'd be pulled back into that world, and he wanted naught to do with it or them. Nor did he want his sire's approval.

His decision was made. He'd go home for a final farewell with the Grants. In the spring, he would visit the Ramsays and ask Logan Ramsay if he could court his daughter.

He swallowed hard at the idea of asking Logan Ramsay for anything at all, but he'd do it.

He loved her.

In the distance, he thought he saw the shape of a cottage, so he slowed his pace and then ducked behind a tree to assess the situation. There were men moving about, but he couldn't see Molly. Two men carrying bundles slipped into the hut, and a third appeared to be climbing a tree, probably an archer.

The archer wasn't there long. A moment later, he fell from the tree, landing at an awkward angle, probably dead. Off to the side, he thought he saw a dark figure crouched behind a tree. *Molly.* He crept forward until he was sure.

Aye. It was his love. He'd find his way to her without startling her. It had taken him a bit longer, but he'd caught up to her.

Now they would finish this together.

◆————○————◆

The sweat on Molly's body collected on her lip, under her arms, between her breasts, and on her hands. She wiped her hands on her tunic to get a better grip. Tormod appeared out of nowhere, sliding up behind her. She held her finger up to her lips to shush him. MacNiven turned around, trying to see them in the dark, but they were still well hidden.

"Tell me the situation," he whispered into her ear.

"One dead, a man named Walrick ran off with Brigid, that way—" she pointed behind the hut, "—and MacNiven is threatening Jennet." Her eyes filled with tears. "Which way do I go? How can I choose?"

"I can feel rumbling in the ground, so your sire comes, I'm sure of it. Go after your sister."

"Are you sure?"

"Aye. You are the fastest. Go, and let me deal with this one."

"But…"

"Take your emotions out of this, warrior, and go after Walrick. He holds your sister and he's on the run. I'll cover you if MacNiven sees you, but he will not."

She leaned over to kiss his lips before chasing off in the direction Walrick had gone, forcing herself to do just as Tormod had told her. How grateful she was to have him by her side, grateful and comforted.

No emotion. That's exactly what would see her through this. She thought of all the trouble that bastard MacNiven had caused her family and her clan. *Enough* was the only word that came to mind.

Enough. She'd save Brigid first, then return for MacNiven and Jennet.

She repeated this in her mind over and over until she had no other thoughts. It took her a while to figure out the trail that Walrick had taken, but she would catch him. She'd been trained by Logan and Gwyneth Ramsay, by the very best, and he would not beat her.

They were her *parents,* her beloved parents.

She had only chased Brigid's kidnapper for a short distance when she caught him. He'd slowed to a walk as he came up to a ravine, a wall of rocks on either side that changed to a ridge on a knoll up ahead. Brigid was still clutched in his one arm, crying softly, but Molly hoped she had not been hurt. Unfortunately, he had climbed the rocks, which made him a more difficult target.

She found a place to hide and pulled out her bow. Halfway up the side of the knoll, he paused to catch his breath.

She nocked and shot her arrow, catching him in his flank. He dropped Brigid and tried to pull the arrow out, but it was lodged deep inside him. The more he pulled, the more his blood flowed.

He collapsed and Brigid sat next to him screaming. Molly raced over and scooped her up, giving her a smile and a kiss on her cheek.

Brigid's eyes were squeezed shut, but she opened them and squealed,

"Molly? 'Tis you, truly? Is he dead?"

Molly glanced at him on the ground. "He's not moving, so we're leaving. I must get you away from him."

"Can you carry me? I hurt my leg. I love you, Molly. Thanks for coming after me."

Molly shifted to try to protect her leg, then started down the hill, but she did not get very far.

A hand grasped her ankle.

CHAPTER TWENTY

MOLLY LOST HER BALANCE AND dropped Brigid as she fell to the ground. "Run, Brigid, run!"

Her sister got up, but while she took a step back, toward the bottom of the ravine, she shouted, "Nay, Molly. I'll not leave you."

All the fear in Molly's body suddenly turned to anger, erupting with a fearsome power. She rolled onto her back so she could look at the villain. His body was covered in blood, but his hand still had a painful grip on her leg.

"I'll kill you before I die, you wee bitch," he growled.

Brigid screamed as his other hand reached up Molly's leg to pull her closer. Her bow was on the ground, but she would not give up so easily. Power collected in her core, and she raised her other leg and kicked him in the face with her boot as hard as she could.

His voice echoed through the ravine. "Arghhhh…I'll kill you." She kicked and squirmed in every direction possible, but he continued to pull her toward him by her left leg. Then she remembered her small dagger.

He was reaching for her throat now, but she still had one leg free—and her dagger was tucked inside her right boot. She kicked and kicked, hoping to push him far enough away for her to grab her knife.

"Molly!" Brigid's scream carried to her, the fear in it reminding her of another sister. When they'd been sent to that cruel English family, she'd been Maggie's protector. She kicked the bastard again and again, throwing fistfuls of dirt at him.

Brigid's cry—*Molly!*—was exactly as heart wrenching as Maggie's had been the first time that cruel woman had taken a switch to her. Tears rolled down Molly's cheeks and she vowed to fight harder…for Brigid… for Maggie…for both her sisters.

She rolled onto her side and grappled at the rocks above her, trying to grab one to use as a weapon, but she couldn't reach it. The attempt cost her. Her attacker had pinned her other leg underneath his large body, which meant she'd never be able to reach her dagger.

"Molly!"

She squirmed in the other direction, and he grabbed her and flipped her underneath him, crawling up her back. Her hand reached out, desperate, and it finally settled on a sizeable rock. Twisting underneath him, she rolled to her side. Pushing away as hard and fast as she could, she swung the rock over her head and brought it down on his temple.

He yelled and fell backward, one hand clutching his head, rolling away from her. His other hand was still hanging on to her left leg, but her right leg was free.

And it was just what she needed. She reached into her boot and grabbed the dagger, swinging it in an arc toward the pulsating vessel in his neck, just as her sire had taught her to do. She plunged it into his skin, sending blood fountaining over her shoulder. As the man's life force left his body, his grip loosened. She kicked away from him, panting to catch her breath as she scrambled down the rocks, tearing the skin on her hand and not caring.

"Brigid?"

"Molly?" Brigid ran to her, and she wrapped her wee sister into a tight embrace, doing her best to calm the lassie's screams of terror while she tried to slow her own breathing.

She glanced over her shoulder at the man who'd attacked her. His life's blood was all around his limp body. She'd never seen so much. He would not be moving again.

"Come, my sweet. We must go for Jennet." She bent down to retrieve her bow.

Molly carried her all the way out of the ravine, and once the ground ahead was clear, she broke into a run.

"Did you save Jennet, too?" the wee lassie hiccuped, clinging to her sister.

"Not yet. But Tormod stayed behind to help her, so I hope he's gotten her by now. We must be quiet when we get near the hut. Can you do that for me? We'll hide behind the rocks until I can see what's happened."

Brigid nodded, doing her best to stop her hiccupping and be quiet already. As they drew closer, Molly slowed her run, taking her time to wind her way through the glen close to the hut. They were still there, MacNiven clutching Jennet close and pressing his knife to her neck. If the blackguard had stood like that the whole time, she wasn't surprised Tormod hadn't acted. He was a good shot, but this would require a perfect hit.

Once she was within shooting range, Molly ducked behind a huge boulder large enough to hide both her and Brigid. She settled her wee sister next to her and out of view. Her heart broke just from looking at the dark circles under her sister's eyes. Brigid and Jennet had been through turmoil, for sure.

Brigid kept her eyes on Molly while she readied her bow. "You'll not leave me, Molly? Please?" She was clutching Molly's tunic, not wanting to let her go.

Molly leaned down and kissed her forehead. "Nay, I'll not go far, but I'll need to step out to fire, so you must let go of me. I may have to go grab Jennet, but you are to stay, understood? I promise to return."

Brigid nodded. "Is your friend still there?"

Molly stuck her head out from behind the rock. She was off to the left of the hut and behind it. Tormod was a little ways to her left, almost even with MacNiven. She hoped he'd noticed her return. Another noise caught her attention. Her sire and three other mounted warriors were now in front of the hut facing her and MacNiven, but she could not hear their discussion, if there was any at all. She leaned down to reassure Brigid. "Da is here, so we will save Jennet." Her sister's eyes brightened and she held her fingers to her lips, letting her know she'd be quiet.

How Molly wished she could confer with her sire, get his opinion on whether shooting would cause MacNiven to cut Jennet. But she could not. She needed to make her own decision, trust her gut.

Her gut said to take MacNiven out now—to take advantage of the distraction her father and the other men would provide.

She hoped his reflex would not cause him to cut Jennet, but since she would shoot to kill, he likely wouldn't be able to put much pressure against her throat.

She would have to chance it.

Leaving her cousin in that madman's hands for one more moment was too risky. She motioned to Tormod, hoping he would see that she intended to shoot. He finally caught sight of her—she could tell by his wide grin and a movement of his hand indicating she should let her arrow fly.

She nocked her arrow and took her time aiming. *Please God, guide my arrow true. Please save my dear cousin.*

Her world slowed, as if the heavens were giving her the time to do everything right. MacNiven turned his head and shoulders to the left as he yelled something she could not hear from her position. Her sire's voice rang, something about MacNiven being a bastard, a lowlife, and a fearful gnat with no courage. He continued his rant, pulling as much emotion as he could from MacNiven, trying to demand his attention.

And she understood why. Her sire knew that forcing MacNiven to look straight at him on his horse would give Molly the target she so desperately needed. But that blackguard had not changed his position enough...

The wounds on her hands stung from grappling on the stones at the ravine, but she had to ignore it. A small breeze moved over her face, almost as if an angel had flown in front of her, telling her now was the time. MacNiven finally turned his body, moving Jennet in front of him, between him and Molly's sire and the other guards, so she was no longer visible to Molly. His body shook as he chuckled, spewing out words that she refused to process. Her entire focus was on Jennet and the bastard who held her hostage, the man who'd attempted to ruin her cousin Torrian's life, who'd planned his murder, who'd tried to kill her cousin Jake, who'd sent his men to kill Ashlyn, and who'd ordered Magnus's death.

The man who'd escaped the king's noose had made a huge mistake. In response to Molly's father's taunting, he finally gave her a full target on his back, so her muscles responded, contracting and releasing in the perfectly choreographed dance she'd practiced for years. She released her arrow, watched it sluice through the air and bury itself in his right flank, exactly where she'd planned to put it—low enough not to accidentally hit Jennet, but in a spot most likely to kill him.

Tormod must have seen her because he unsheathed his sword and ran straight for the villain as soon as her arrow hit his flank.

MacNiven bellowed and stumbled backwards, dragging Jennet with him. The wee lassie surprised all of them by biting into his hand. He dropped the dagger, but his grip on Jennet didn't weaken. Holding her tight—then tighter—he fell onto the ground, using his feet to push himself out of view of the warriors' horses.

He was losing a lot of blood, but he wouldn't release Jennet. It was a choking, punishing grip.

Jennet screamed, clawing at the man's hand, but to no avail. Tormod reached them and pushed Jennet away so he could put his sword through the man's belly. Still, he did not release Jennet. Tormod put his foot on MacNiven's chest for leverage and tugged at his hand. When Molly reached them, she gathered up Jennet, trying to release her. MacNiven's eyes were glazing over, and when Tormod gave one last heave against MacNiven's claw-like hand, Jennet finally fell into Molly's hands, crying and clutching her cousin.

Logan reached them first and kissed both Molly and Jennet before shouting, "Well done. Brigie? Where's Brigie?"

Molly held Jennet close as she pointed to the rock behind her. "Over there, Papa. She hurt her leg is all." She yelled over her shoulder, "Brigie, come on out, sweetie, it's safe."

Gwyneth rode up to them, in a panic Molly had never seen before. "She's hale, Molly? Jennet? You are all right?"

Torrian followed fast behind her on his mount. "Jennet?"

Jennet left Molly and ran to her brother, who lifted her up onto his lap, hugging her close. Logan came out from behind the rock with Brigid, whose arms were locked about his neck. He handed her over to Gwyneth, who immediately broke into sobs. "Thank you, Lord. Oh my, thank you, Lord."

Tormod reached over to brush the dirt off Molly's face. "Well done, lass."

Molly's gaze locked on his, and she was oblivious to all else that was happening around them. Tormod had supported her, encouraged her, and believed in her. She couldn't stop the broad smile that crossed her face as she stared into his blue eyes. "We did it, did we not?"

His grin almost matched hers. "Nay, *you* did. You single-handedly saved Brigid, and you put an arrow in MacNiven's back, stopping him from cutting Jennet's throat."

"But *your* blow was the killing blow, and your hand freed her. We did this together."

He leaned over and gave her a chaste kiss on her lips. "Aye, I guess we did."

They stood there for a long moment, staring at each other, smiling, and then Logan came over and pulled Molly into a hug. "Well done. The king is here, and he promised to follow directly behind us. He wishes to see MacNiven himself."

"How did you find us, Papa?" Molly asked.

"Davina told us everything she knew. I feel sorry for the poor lass. She hasn't led an easy life."

Molly nodded. "Aye. She's the one who told us where to go. We must thank her. I do not know what would have happened had we not come upon them so quickly."

Logan said, "You may send her a message later. I believe the king said her sire was on his way to bring her home. If not, he would have his warriors escort her home, just as he was sending some guards along with Cedrica and Lorna to Edinburgh. One of them has a relative there."

Taking her hand in his and turning it over, Tormod said, "You had a bit of a battle with Walrick, I see. Your hands are a mess."

"You had to use your dagger, lass?" her sire whispered as he used his plaid to wipe some of the blood from her face.

"Aye." She leaned into Tormod as he wrapped his arm around her shoulder. "I hit him with my arrow in his flank, but he did not die. He grabbed my ankle when I picked up Brigid from where she'd fallen."

Her sire leaned in to kiss her cheek. "So proud of you, lassie." Clasping Tormod's shoulder, he said, "You two work well together. As worried as I was throughout this entire episode, naught struck me worse than when MacNiven squeezed Jennet like that after he dropped the dagger. My heart dropped to the bottom of my belly. My thanks for freeing her from his death grip."

The king's bellow interrupted their small celebration. He dismounted in front of Molly and Tormod. "And are these the warriors I must thank, Ramsay? This fine lass is your daughter, is she not?"

Logan turned to the king. "Aye, this is my eldest daughter, Molly."

"Is this not the one I gave to you from the English fop?"

"Aye, we adopted her with your blessing. She has a sister Maggie at home." His face beamed with pride.

"And the young lad?"

"Tormod Moriston, of the Grant clan, taught by some of the best, as you know."

"Bring me to the devil's body. I need to see it myself."

Logan had been standing in front of the body to hide it from the lassies' view, so he stood back to allow the king to see him.

"It gives me great satisfaction to see this issue ended," the king said with a sigh. Then he turned to face Molly and Tormod. "Aye, many thanks to the two of you. I'm sure you will wish to celebrate with your clan after this, and I'll be sure to send the best wine and food along." He glanced down at the ground and then took a few steps away from them in order to kick the dead body that now lay at his feet. "Ranulf MacNiven, you'll cause my countrymen no more trouble."

He glanced behind him at Jennet, who was still sitting on the horse with her brother. "Aye, Torrian? Does this not please you? And Jennet, my wee friend—" he moved over to pat her leg, "—you are well? The Scots still need you to grow into a fine healer like your mother and her sister Jennie."

"I am well, my king. How has the ache in your hand been?" Despite the horrors she had narrowly survived, Jennet had already slipped back into healer mode.

Jennet had tended the king's hand while on that long-ago visit to Edinburgh. Even before she'd unwittingly revealed MacNiven's ruse, she'd softened the king to their clan. Wee Jennet was so much like Aunt Brenna.

King Alexander guffawed. "You are a true healer, lass. My hand is much better, thank you. You are a strong lass to have survived such a thing."

Her mother pulled her horse over next to Torrian's, Brigid still on her lap. "My king," the wee lassie said, her eyes wide, "Jennet told him she was a witch and they were all afraid of her."

King Alexander said, "That was a wise move, my dear. Many grown men are afraid of witches, though my wee Jennet is certainly not one."

Gwyneth asked, "And my niece left us messages. If she hadn't, we might never have tracked them down."

The king frowned. "What say you? I have not heard of this."

"My cousin left us messages by carving them into the bark of trees," Molly said, smiling at her cousin. "She told us which direction they were traveling."

"My, but aren't you clever lassies! You helped us catch a man who has been on the run for quite some time. What made you think of that, Jennet?"

"My mama. She showed us how to leave the messages, and she once told us a tale of a lass pretending to be a witch, so I did the same."

"Hmmm," King Alexander said, his finger tapping on his lower lip.

"I believe I'll send you some more of my special oranges as a reward for staying strong."

Brigid clapped and Jennet's eyes widened.

"I'll send them special delivery, one for each of you. Now off with you, Jennet. I know a mother and father who would like to see you at home." The king spoke to Gwyneth. "All is well with your injury?"

Gwyneth replied, "I am much better, though both my daughter and I seem to have sore legs."

"Then home with you both. There are many there to care for you. You both deserve a rest and my thanks. You make me proud to be a Scot."

He almost stepped on the archer's body who had fallen out of the tree. "And who is this, Ramsay? Who is the fool who lost his life following a halfwit?"

Logan moved over to the king's side. "I do not recognize him."

A halting voice came from behind him. "I do."

Logan swung around and gave Molly a surprised look. "You do?"

"Aye. He's the man who attacked me at the royal castle during the celebration. The one who pushed me down the passageway and punched me in the back. He is wearing the same clothing and is about the right size. Remember, Papa?"

Logan whispered, "I do. It all fits, does it not?" He wrapped his arm around her shoulder and squeezed her tight. "So proud of you, daughter. You knew exactly what I was doing when I was yelling at MacNiven."

"Aye, you gave me the perfect target."

He hugged her tight. "I knew you could do it. Many thanks for saving the lassies."

Tormod came up behind her. "She's a quick runner."

"Aye, she is one of the fastest. I do not know how you kept up with her, Moriston, but you did well."

"But I did..."

Molly interrupted him. "He supported me, Papa. I was not sure I could do this without you or Mama at my side, but he encouraged me from start to finish."

Logan clasped Tormod's shoulder and whispered, "Nicely done. Let's take our leave from this horrid place."

CHAPTER TWENTY-ONE

TORMOD STARED AT UP AT the evening sky that had turned a beautiful blue with a touch of purple across the wispy clouds. While the king had promised to send his men back to clean up the MacNiven castle, he'd ordered the Ramsay contingency to head home.

The first night, they'd ridden just a few hours before making camp for the night. While they had all been jubilant at first, exhaustion had settled in on them and Logan had ordered them to make the stop. The conditions hadn't been the best, but everyone had been too tired to care. There was a cave for the women to sleep in, and the men slept in the front.

By morn, a contingent from the king had brought them gifts—his traveling tent and baskets of bread and cheeses to take with them on their journey.

Jamie had come up to speak to Tormod at first light, asking him whether he was ready to head back to Grant land. The snow had been light this year, and the king had informed him that he thought the weather would allow them to return.

Tormod had stared at Jamie, feeling a little shocked by the thought of it. He hadn't considered the possibility they would return so soon.

"I had guessed you might feel that way. Molly means a lot to you, does she not?" Jamie had tipped his head to the side, letting a slow grin move across his face. "I'm happy for you."

How correct Jamie had been. Molly was so much more to him than a warrior in his clan, and he was not ready to part ways yet. Maybe not ever. "Mayhap I'll visit Ramsay land in the spring and..." He struggled with what to do or say, but then Jamie had thought of exactly the right solution.

"If you think you can live without seeing your sire and brother until spring, I'd suggest you go with the Ramsays and see what you wish to do about it. Do not rush into aught, but what you've found with Molly is worth exploring."

"My sire?" He snorted. "I can live without my sire until spring."

Jamie patted his shoulder. "I thought so. Speak to my uncle before you go any further, but given all you've done for his family, I doubt he'll turn you away."

"But I'm not sure if I'm ready to...to..."

"You do not need to be sure of your feelings for Molly, but spending the winter in Grant land will not help you sort them out."

They were quiet for a moment, and Logan, who had an uncanny ability to read situations, came up beside them. "By the way, lad," he said, clapping Tormod on the back, "you're welcome to spend time with the Ramsays if you're not interested in the long journey back to Grant land in the middle of winter. 'Tis a much nicer journey in springtime."

"Many thanks. I accept."

Jamie quirked his brow and waited for Logan to walk away. "Braden, Coll, and I will leave the trail in a couple of hours. Best of luck to you."

That had been several hours ago, and right before Jamie had left, he'd said, "I'll make sure your sire and brother hear of all your exploits, right down to delivering the killing blow to the very villain the king has chased for many moons. Lyall will have naught to say by the time we get done explaining how you put your sword into MacNiven's belly to save a wee lass."

Coll and Braden had added, "We'll have a good time making sure your brother knows how well you did on this journey."

They had parted ways, and Tormod had no regrets. He'd spent the next couple of hours thinking about his past—and what he hoped for in his future.

One was that he had no regrets. He was not going home anytime soon, and he did not care. True, he would have enjoyed seeing the look on his sire's face when he heard of his accomplishments, but the idea had lost most of its appeal.

He no longer cared what his sire thought of what he'd done. He was more interested in hearing what his laird thought.

All because of Molly Ramsay.

Molly Ramsay had changed him forever. He still could not believe how gracefully she'd covered for him. He'd been on the verge of admitting that he hadn't kept pace with her, but she hadn't let him do it. And then she'd lauded him for everything he'd done to support her.

He trusted her, which didn't come easily for him. It was one of the reasons he'd fallen in love with her. When it had happened, he couldn't be sure, but he was sure that he never wanted to be apart from her again.

It came time to stop for the second night, and Logan led them off the main trail and into a clearing. Tormod dismounted, took care of his needs and his horse, and then searched for Logan. Now that he'd started imagining a future with Molly, he no longer wanted to wait.

Logan and his wife were sitting on a log on one side of the clearing, and fortunately, Molly was not with them. Brigid and Jennet were not far away, but he thought this was his chance. He strode over to them and asked, "May I have a moment of your time, my lord?"

Logan stood up, though Gwyneth stayed on the log because of her leg. "What is it, lad?"

"I wanted, that is—" he wiped the sweat from his palms onto his trews under his plaid. He might as well just say it. "I would like to ask for your daughter's hand in marriage. That is…if she's not promised to another."

He waited what seemed like an eternity while Logan looked him up and down, and then shot a glance at his wife. He thought Gwyneth gave her husband a nod and a smile, but he could not be certain.

"And if you'll allow me, I'd like to ask her myself privately, if you approve." He coughed and shuffled his feet, wanting more than anything to pace, but he knew that would be wrong.

Logan took two steps forward until he stood directly in front of Tormod, so close he only needed to whisper. "You have our permission, lad. Naught would please us more, but understand that Molly's early life was most difficult. She has never had any interest in marrying up until this point, and she may never marry. Understand that Molly is quite special."

He let out the breath he'd been holding. "I know Molly is special, and she has shared some of her memories with me. I promise to treat her with care if she'll have me."

"You do that. In fact, you may start now. She's gone off by herself for a few moments. She wished to watch the sunset, something she does whenever she can." He pointed off in the distance. "She went in that direction."

Tormod had a hard time containing his relief. He nodded to Gwyneth and then took off after her. Once he got past the trees, he saw her standing and staring up at the beautiful sunset, the purples and blues even more beautiful with Molly silhouetted against it. He broke into a run and made it almost to her side before she spun around.

Molly stared up at the beautiful sky, her mind still lost in the wonderful dream she'd had the night before. How she wished her Aunt Lina were here so she could ask her some questions, but she'd be with her soon enough.

In the dream, she and Tormod were married. They were traveling by horseback together in the middle of a warm summer day, and both of them were so very happy. The love she had for him washed over her as they cantered through a field of deep heather. At one point, they broke into a gallop and she could not stop laughing, her hair unbound and flowing in the wind.

She could not decide if it had been a dream or a vision. The aura of it had made her think it was a vision, which was what she *wanted* to believe, but something else told her it could only be a dream.

Why? She had looked pretty in the dream. She'd avoided any hint of her reflection for years, knowing that she would only see the plain lass her birth sire had ridiculed, but in this dream, she'd been pretty. And Tormod? He'd been so handsome it had taken her breath away.

A sound interrupted her thoughts. She twirled around to catch Tormod headed straight for her, a smile on his face.

"Tormod. I'm glad you're here. Is the sunset not the most beautiful one you've ever seen? Last night's was pretty, but this one is stunning."

"Aye, it is." He took one look at her and did what he'd been dying to do all day. He kissed her, a deep kiss—a kiss that he hoped reflected how much he cared for her. She parted her lips for him and he tasted her, teasing her with his tongue until she gave a small squeak.

He ended the kiss, too nervous to continue. "Molly, I spoke with your mother and father, and they gave me permission."

"Permission for what?"

He took her hand in his, lacing his fingers with hers. "Molly, why did you stop me when I was about to tell your sire that I could not keep up with you?"

She reached up to cup his cheek with one hand, brushing her thumb across his rough stubble. "You did not need to say it. You kept up with me in so many other ways. You encouraged me the whole way, building me up every chance you could, and that meant far more to me than running alongside me would have. You were the one who convinced me I could do it on my own without my mother, and without you, I may not have been able to do it."

"Molly? I'm not verra good at this, but I know that I want you by my side for the rest of my life. I feel complete when I'm with you. I know that does not sound right, but I don't know how else to explain it. The thought of going back to Grant land and leaving you…I…I *never* want to leave you. I love you with all my heart. Would you, will you…will you marry me?"

She jumped into his arms and said, "Aye, I will. I love you, too, Tormod."

He kissed her again, a deep kiss to let her know how much he loved her and how pleased he was to hear her declare her love for him. His chest swelled with happiness.

They were going to marry.

She stepped back, but while her arms were still wrapped around his waist, a very serious expression adorned her features. "But I must ask, where do you wish to live? You are part of the Grant clan, and I am part of the Ramsay clan. They are not neighboring lands."

Her shoulders slumped, and he guessed she was worried about leaving her family, so he took her hand and found a rock for them to sit on. "Come and we'll talk."

She followed him, her hand still laced with his, her face beaming. The thought of waking up to see her in his arms every morning made him more excited for the future than anything ever had.

"Molly, if you approve, I would ask permission to join your clan. What matters most to me is for us to be together. Naught else is important."

"You would?" she asked, her eyes filling with light and excitement. "That makes me so happy, Tormod. You know not how that eases my mind. I do not know if I could bear to leave my family. But would you not miss yours? You have a father and a brother, aye?"

"Aye, but I like the idea of starting over. My brother…" he stared off into space, unsure of whether or not to tell her the truth, but she was to be his wife, and when they traveled back to Grant land to visit the clan of his birth, she would hear his story anyway. He brought his gaze back to hers and was so humbled by the love he saw in her eyes that he forged ahead.

"When I was younger, my brother and his wife did something that humiliated me..." He gave her a short explanation without going into great detail.

"Tormod, how terrible that your own brother would embarrass you so," she said, reaching up to touch his cheek. "Why would he do such a thing?"

"I know not. I tell you this not for your pity, but because I want you to know why 'tis easy for me to leave my family. I am quite sure they will not miss me at all. I lost my mother at a young age, and I will forever love and miss her, but now..." His gaze drifted off again. This was what he needed to do. Someday he would return to Grant land for a visit, but not until Molly was his wife. With her by his side, he would be able to handle the taunts he'd so often received, but for now, he tired of them.

"Now, I wish to build a new life with my wife. I do not wish for my family's interference."

"Do you think they would? Would they not like me?"

"My sire would love you, but being with you has made me believe in myself, and I do not wish to return to my old life. We'll start anew, together, if you agree."

"Naught would make me happier, Tormod."

They both heard feet moving toward them, and Molly rose from the rock. Her father was standing there with a grin on his face. Her mother, whom he was carrying in his arms, was smiling just as widely.

"Well?" they said in tandem.

Molly laughed, clutching onto Tormod's hand and leaning into his side. "We're getting married."

CHAPTER TWENTY-TWO

TORMOD WAS PLEASED TO HEAR the Ramsay whoop as soon as they crossed into Ramsay land. They hadn't gone far before Quade Ramsay, surrounded by fifteen guards, rode toward them at full speed, only slowing when he drew near. He headed straight for Torrian's horse, and Torrian slowed enough to hand Jennet over to her father.

"Papa!" rang out across the hills. Jennet threw herself into her father's arms, and Tormod would wager he saw some tears in the corners of Quade Ramsay's eyes. He also caught the silent, respectful warrior's nod exchanged between father and son. Quade's eyes closed in what appeared to be a silent prayer of thanks.

Tormod glanced over at Molly, riding abreast of him, and was not surprised to see tears flowing down her cheeks.

"No problems, lass?" He had feared her headaches would return on the journey, but she had denied any recurrence.

She shook her head, smiling, as the rest of the Ramsay guards joined them. As they continued to ride toward the keep, the Ramsay war whoop echoed through the trees, announcing to those who awaited in the castle that their journey had been successful.

After the third war whoop, Tormod decided to try his own version of the Ramsay whoop with the others. It was much different from the Grant whoop, and he could hear Molly's giggle beside him.

Fortunately, his new laird did not tell him to stop. Torrian only smiled at him.

When they were just outside the gates, one horse emerged, followed by two mounted guards. He knew the rider to be a female because her unbound hair waved in the breeze behind her. When she was almost upon them, she stopped her horse and dismounted, heading directly for Quade Ramsay's horse.

Lady Brenna, sobbing for all to hear, tore across the field toward her daughter. Quade stopped the procession with one hand, then lowered Jennet from the horse so she could run into her mother's arms, a sweet "Mama," erupting from her.

Lady Brenna fell to the ground, rocking her wee one in her arms, unable to stop her tears. Quade motioned the others on toward the keep, but he stayed back with several guards. It was a homecoming Tormod would never forget.

Once they were all gathered inside, delighted chatter filled the great hall. Tormod and Molly were motioned to sit at the dais with Quade, Logan, and Torrian. Gwyneth stayed by the hearth with Brenna and the wee ones.

"Tell me so I can hear it with my own ears," Quade said. "MacNiven is dead?"

Logan nodded. "Three of them branched off with the girls: MacNiven, his second Walrick, and an unknown archer. Molly put arrows in all three of them, but while her shot killed the archer, she had to use her dagger to finish Walrick, and Tormod put his sword in MacNiven's belly in order to remove the blackguard's death grip from Jennet."

"And Bearchun and Shaw?"

"Unfortunately, no answer there. They have not been seen since Jennet made him drop to the ground by cutting her hand and holding her blood up in front of his face. Your daughter convinced all but MacNiven she was a witch."

"That's my wee lassie." Quade grinned from ear to ear as he gazed over at his wife and daughters. "And where were you and Torrian during all this?"

They told him a short version of the whole tale, then Torrian interjected, "And do tell him the most important, Uncle Logan," Torrian prompted, tipping his head toward Tormod and Molly.

"Of course, I was getting to that."

Quade glanced back and forth between the two of them. "What?"

"Tormod and Molly are marrying, and Tormod wishes to join our clan."

Tormod stood up, almost knocking his chair over. "With your acceptance of course, my lord. I placed my request to your chief, and he approved." He tipped his head toward Torrian. "I ask with the utmost respect for Clan Grant, but I am in love with your niece and we wish to marry and live here."

Quade grinned. "Wonderful. And may I assume that the Grants support your wishes?"

"Aye," Logan replied, "Jamie said they would."

Tormod pivoted to face Logan. "You asked, my lord?" He must have done so before Tormod had even asked for her hand.

Logan laughed. "Aye, I've seen the way you look at my daughter, lad."

Quade clasped his hands in front of him. "Then you better marry her quick, before you give my brother a reason to fight you. He does not like lads touching his daughters over much."

Tormod turned a pale shade of green.

Ever since they'd returned, Molly had listened to nothing but conversations about her wedding, the celebration, and what she would wear. She decided she had to put an end to it. She just couldn't go through with what her mother, aunts, and sisters wanted. Tormod had said he was happy to do whatever she'd like, so it was time to let everyone else know what she'd decided.

Molly dreaded what she was about to do, but she had no choice. She had to stay true to who she was, and that meant she could not do what everyone else wished her to do.

Aye, she'd marry Tormod because she loved him, because he completed her. He gave her comfort some days, yet excited her beyond belief on others. But a wedding dress? Aye, her sire had told her that her mother had donned a wedding dress, but she'd done it for his mother, and Molly's grandmother was no longer here. Of course, Uncle Rab, who was also the priest who would perform the ceremony, would be a bit more difficult to convince, but first she needed to talk with her mother and sisters.

She opened the door to the chamber where her mother and the other lasses in the clan had been gathering to discuss the wedding, and took a deep breath for strength. She was surprised to see only her mother and her sister Maggie.

Gwyneth took her hands and pulled her over to the table with the fabrics laid carefully on display. "Look at the choices you have. Aunt

Brenna had just ordered new fabric. You'll be lovely, but the color is your choice."

"Mama." Molly tugged her hand away from her mother's.

"What is it?"

Molly stared at the floor, tears brimming at the corners of her eyes

Maggie whispered, "It's as I warned you, Mama. She will not want this, and 'tis all our true sire's fault."

Gwyneth lifted her daughter's chin so that their gazes met, and waited for her explanation. It was time to free the words that had been weighing down her tongue. "Mama, Tormod and I have discussed this, and we would prefer to be married quietly by Uncle Rab alone somewhere, or just with you and Da and my sisters and brothers. We do not wish to have a big celebration, or for all the clan to come from afar for the wedding. We'd prefer something simple."

"But the clan looks forward to the celebrations whenever a member of the chieftain's family marries. There's always food for everyone. There will be dancing and minstrels and…"

Molly turned her head trying to hide her tears. How could she do such a thing? She could not bear to hear the things that would be said about her.

Maggie grabbed her by the shoulders and said, "Now you listen to me. I have always been with you, and I was there in that hut when Papa insulted you." Her sister was as fierce as she was beautiful.

Gwyneth turned to Maggie. "What are you referring to? I know he did not think he could find anyone to marry her because of her looks, but…"

Maggie ignored her mother and continued. "I recall the name he called you, and he was wrong. Molly, when you were younger, you were so thin that you were gangly, but you were never homely. He treated you abominably. You must remove it from your mind."

"What did he call you?" Gwyneth's wide eyes caused the tears to flow even harder.

"Maggie, please do not tell her, do not tell anyone. Please," Molly begged her sister. "I know what I look like, and I know I'm not beautiful." She turned to her mother. "Do you not understand? I do not wish to go through this. The horrid names he called me do not matter, but I have experienced all that I care to of people talking behind their hands, waiting until I walk away to insult me. People will continue to talk about my homely looks for my entire life, but I do not wish to encourage them. Walking in front of a crowd will invite the stares, the looks of pity. Please. I do not wish to go through it again, and I have been fortunate enough to find someone that loves me for who I am. Do not force me to subject myself to such humiliation for the good of the clan. I cannot take it!"

Molly spun on her heel and ran for the door, but for once her sister was faster. Leaning over her from behind, Maggie held the door shut no matter how she tugged. "That is enough from you. I have allowed you to ignore the truth all our lives because I recall what you went through, but it is done. No more. Mama? Grab the packages. I will drag her outside to the caves and prove it to her."

Molly did her best to get away, but Maggie would not let her go, and when she looked to her mother for assistance, Gwyneth just smiled and said, "I agree with your sister. You'll go with us willingly, or I will call your sire and brothers to drag you outside. You will listen to us alone, out near the caves, for one hour. If at that time, you still wish to marry quietly, I will agree. But you must willingly go with us for one hour." She folded her arms in front of her chest and waited for a response.

"If 'twill put an end to this, then I agree. One hour. The sun is falling, so I am watching."

Maggie smiled and led her out the door and down the steps. Molly sighed, frustrated at their stubbornness, but if this would put an end to all their ridiculous talk, then she could bear it for one hour.

She followed her sister, ignoring the stares from the clanmates as they passed. They stared at her the same way they would if she married with all of them watching. How she wished Tormod was with her. "Where's Da? Why is he not here with you?" She glared at her mother.

"Your sire is not coming. You always twist the man to your side of things. He is too soft-hearted."

Maggie stopped in front of the cave where they and their sisters had played in many times as bairns. They loved it, yet it frightened them because it was so dark and shiny, often appearing wet when the stone was dry. There were times when they'd given themselves chills by imagining they could see a scary ghost in the dark stone. Molly plopped onto the grass between the cave and the trees off to the right, picking up sticks and tossing them.

Maggie held her hand out to their mother, waited until she set something in her hand, then marched over to Molly and handed her the package. "This is from Uncle Rab, who sent for this many moons ago for you. He wished to give it to you someday for your wedding gift, but you need to open it now. He has given me permission to allow you to open it early."

Molly scowled, but took the package, gingerly opening the twine wrapped around the small parcel that was about as large as a man's hand. Inside she found a small box, so she took the cover off and lifted out a piece of metal. Setting it on her lap, she looked up at her mother, confused. She had no idea what it was.

"Turn it over," her mother advised.

She turned it over to find a shiny piece of metal on the other side of the square. "What is it?" She looked from her sister to her mother, hoping one of them would give her some guidance because she'd never seen anything like this fey, shiny thing. "And where did Uncle Rab get it?"

"My brother heard about them from a traveling priest," her mother said, reaching over to touch her cheek. "He said they had such things in France and Venice, Italy, so he paid for the priest to bring him one when he visited again. That was two years ago. He arrived a moon ago, and brought it with him."

"Uncle Rab did that for me?"

"Aye, because Uncle Rab knows how tender your heart is."

Maggie sat next to her and said, "Hold it in front of you." She guided Molly's hand until the square was directly in front of her face.

Her mother whispered, "What do you see?"

Molly looked at the metal and noticed something she hadn't seen before. The metal was so shiny it reflected an image back at her. She could see eyes, a nose, and a chin as clear as day. "Maggie, I see you." She stood up because she was so surprised. She held it over to her mother. "Look, Mama. It's Maggie. Is she not beautiful?"

Her mother glanced at Maggie with a smile on her face. "You are correct, daughter. She has no idea."

"I told you, Mama. Even when the loch is as clear as glass, she refuses to look at herself. She always has. Whenever Sorcha and I find a plate or a bowl we can see ourselves in, Molly always leaves. She has never looked at herself."

"I do not wish to see myself. If I do, I'll forever be reminded of my sire." And she'd forever be reminded of how ugly she was, ugly as a goat—just as her father had reminded her often enough.

A goat, a gray, hairy-chinned goat. She could not stop herself from rubbing her chin as she had done every time he'd called her that, just to see if she had hair there.

Well, she would rather not see herself. So long as she avoided her reflection, she could pretend that she was as pretty as everyone else. If she saw her ugly reflection in the loch, it would be locked there forever.

Did they not understand that?

"What does my looking at myself in the loch have to do with this wedding?"

Maggie stood and moved over to settle her hands on her sister's shoulders. "Because, Molly, I've tried to tell you many times how beautiful you are, but you do not believe me."

Her mother stood behind Maggie, nodding her head. "All true. I've witnessed it many times."

"The metal," Maggie said. "'Tis not me you see in the metal, Molly. That beautiful lass is you."

Molly's eyes widened as her heart jumped to her throat. Could she be telling the truth? She brought the shiny metal back up to her face only because there was something that rang true about her sister's words. While the image she'd seen in the metal looked a bit like Maggie, it was not Maggie, but someone else.

She held it up so she could look again.

The lass she saw was beautiful, and it was neither her mother nor Maggie. When her lips moved, the same thing happened in the image. If she turned her head, the girl in the image did, too. Her hand flew up to her mouth because something hit her, something that was beyond belief.

She, Molly Ramsay, was not the ugly beast her true sire had always mocked her for being. Her brown eyes were fringed by long lashes, her hair curled down her back—and it actually looked quite beautiful when she turned sideways to see it.

"Smile, daughter," her mother whispered from over her shoulder.

She smiled, and her eyes filled with tears. Her teeth were white and straight, and she was...

"Oh my goodness. I'm pretty." She turned to Maggie and threw her arms around her neck. "I'm truly pretty! My thanks, Maggie."

She hugged her mother. "Do you not agree, Mama? I am pretty, am I not?"

Her mother stood back and cupped her cheeks. "Sweeting, you are beautiful. You have rosy cheeks and white teeth and pink lips. Your hair is stunning and long. You *are* beautiful, believe it. Now—" she reached for another package, "—I brought this gown along for you to try on. There is a lovely surcoat with it. Please try it."

"But I'll not be able to see it in this small image."

Maggie tugged her over to the wall of the cave. "You can see yourself in here. This black stone will show you. 'Tis just the right time of day to see yourself."

Molly searched the area but found no one, so she stripped out of her plaid and tunic and leggings. Her mother helped her don the pale blue undergown and the surcoat over it, a soft green shot through with blue and gold threads. Maggie tugged her by the hand over to the black shiny rock embedded on the side of the cave.

"What do you think?" Maggie whispered, her chin resting on her sister's shoulder.

Molly burst into tears, sobbing her heart out at the vision she saw in the rock.

Molly Ramsay was beautiful.

CHAPTER TWENTY-THREE

THE MORNING OF MOLLY'S WEDDING, a light knock sounded at her door. She'd just finished dressing and was waiting to hear from her mother about what to do next.

"Enter," she called out.

The door opened slowly, and a dear face peeked into the room.

"Uncle Rab!" She jumped up from her chair and threw her arms around her uncle. Rab was her mother's only family, and she loved him dearly.

He kissed her cheek and stood back, glancing at her from head to toe. "Och, but you have become quite a beauty, niece."

"Thanks to you, Uncle Rab. You have no idea how much your gift meant to me. Many thanks."

"You're welcome. But you did not need a shiny piece of metal to be beautiful, lass."

She sat on the bed and tugged him down next to her. "I know, Uncle. Tormod always told me I was beautiful, and I never believed him, but the funny thing is that I believed Tormod *thought* I was beautiful. It surprised me to see that I was much prettier than I'd ever believed. Thank you, Uncle Rab."

"You have always had the biggest heart, child. You protected your wee sisters, Sorcha and Maggie, like a bear would protect her cubs. And then you became the protector of wee Jennet and Brigid, too. We are all indebted to your big heart. I said more prayers after those two lassies were stolen than I ever have. I wore a hole in my kneeler that the clan ladies covered with a cushion for me."

"Uncle Rab, I do love you so, and I'm grateful you'll be marrying us today."

He held his arm out for her. "May I escort my dear niece to the chapel?"

"I would love to have you escort me."

He kissed her cheek and held the door for her. Once in the passage-way, he held his arm out to her, and she took hold of it, smiling as they made their way down the stairs and into the great hall where her mother and father awaited her.

Her father held out his arm. "I believe 'tis my job, as well, lass. You are as lovely as I knew you would be."

Maggie and Sorcha joined her on one side while her mother and Brigid joined her on the other. They moved down the stairs outside the keep to a chorus of cheers from their clanmates. Gavin lifted her onto her horse and Rab and her sire led the horse to the chapel. Cousin Torrian, her laird, and his sire, Uncle Quade, sat on their destriers on either side of the courtyard in a kind of salute to the wedding.

Molly heard the comments from some of the clan.

"Is she not beautiful?"

"Look at how lovely her hair is."

"Her gown is stunning. She has turned into a fine-looking lass, has she not?"

Molly could not stop smiling, still unaccustomed to such flattery and compliments. When she was almost to the chapel, she saw Tormod standing in front of it, and the sight of him simply took her breath away. Dressed in a white leine and the blue and black Ramsay plaid, he was the most handsome man there. His hand fussed with the sword sheathed at his side, indicating he was as nervous as she was about what was to come.

Once her sire stopped the horse, Uncle Rab nodded and stepped inside the chapel to take his place at the altar. Tormod hurried over to help her dismount, his hands reaching for her waist, but a low growl erupted from her sire's chest as he shoved Tormod aside and grabbed Molly's waist, uttering a curt, "Not yet, lad," that caused everyone within hear-ing distance to burst into laughter. She rolled her eyes at her father, but then kissed his cheek before he escorted her inside, Tormod following them.

Once everyone had taken their places, Molly and Tormod moved to the front of the chapel with her uncle. She was so nervous, she hardly heard any of Father Rab's words—her focus was entirely on the man she loved, who was standing beside her, his hand entwined with hers. Every once in a while, he would glance down at her and her heart would flutter, just as it always had whenever he was nearby. How she hoped for a marriage as strong as her parents' union.

As soon as she knelt for a prayer, the first thing she did was thank God for her mother and father finding her in Edinburgh; for all her siblings, her aunts, uncles, and cousins; and for sending Tormod to her. For a quick moment, she was back inside her true parents' home, listening to her father berate her mother, but she dashed that image away by glancing over her shoulder at her adoptive sire, Logan Ramsay, who had taught her so much. He winked at her. Her mother had tears in her eyes as she squeezed Logan's arm.

A small piece of her wished her true mother could see her now, but it wasn't to be. Her mother had loved her; she believed that with all her heart.

Tormod squeezed her hand, bringing her back to the present and the ceremony, and she beamed at him.

When the time finally came for the end of the ceremony and the kiss, Molly surprised herself by throwing her arms around Tormod's neck and kissing him with all her heart.

When they sat at the table on the dais, watching the revelry, Molly leaned over and whispered in Tormod's ear, "Husband, you have not told me what is to happen this eve."

She knew what was to take place, but she wished to hear it from Tormod, whom she trusted implicitly. Her younger brother had taught her about the male anatomy, especially because she and Maggie had both learned the hard way to stand back when changing the laddie's rags. Along with her cousins, she'd delighted in talking about making bairns for many years. Lily was especially delightful in the way she spoke of the act. She had not hesitated to tell her cousins that lovemaking was one of the most wonderful parts of marriage.

Her mother had also talked to her about the wedding night. Gwyneth Ramsay did not have a shy bone in her body and had been quite explicit. Secretly, Molly had been pleased because she preferred to be prepared for any circumstance. But while she understood the basics, she was confused about some of the specifics. The intimacy of it was a bit frightening to her.

Tormod quirked a brow at her. "Have I not told you yet? Well, allow me to fix that error now."

"Here?" Molly had only sought to tease Tormod. She didn't expect him to start telling her anything on the dais, though everyone else was presently dancing or chatting and they were alone together. They'd married within a sennight of returning to Ramsay land, so they hadn't had much opportunity to even do much kissing.

It didn't help that Molly's father had taken to growling at Tormod anytime he had come near her.

"If I have my way, I plan to carry you up the stairs to your chamber." Stopping to frown for a moment, he said, "They have given us our own chamber for the night, have they not?"

She nodded, giggling. "Please continue."

He wrapped his arm around her waist and continued. "While I carry you, there's naught I would love more than to cup my hand on your sweet bottom, caressing you as I carry you slowly down the passageway…"

Molly leaned into him and he moved his mouth next to her ear. "I cannot wait to feel your skin against mine. If I could, I'd lift your skirts while I carried you and slip my hand underneath the undergown so I could…"

"And I will like it?"

"You tell me." He continued to stare out at the crowd mingling and bouncing to the music, but she felt a draft of air under her skirt followed by a hand settling against her upper leg…a very *warm* hand.

"Tormod…" she whispered.

"Hush, act like naught is happening. The tablecloth your aunt placed across the dais reaches the floor. No one but you knows what I am doing."

She nodded, glancing first at the tablecloth and feeling it with her toe, just to be sure he was correct, but then she focused all her attentions on his hand.

"Do you like it?"

"Aye, I do," her voice came out in a husky tone, and she grabbed his forearm under the table.

"Do you wish for me to stop?"

"Nay."

His hand caressed the inside of her thigh, up and down, sneaking up higher and higher. "Your skin is just as soft as I knew it would be."

Her grip tightened on his forearm. She was unsure about all the feelings she was experiencing, but she did not stop him. Her cousin Lily had told her that if she relaxed, she would love it, even though it would hurt a bit the first time.

"We're at our chamber. What do you do now?" She fluttered her lashes at him, shocked at her own behavior.

"I'll carry you across the threshold and lay you down on the bed... Nay, I've changed my mind. I'll set you on your feet instead."

"Why did you change your mind?"

"Because I wish to see all of you. I'll light several candles so I can see how beautiful you are. First, I will ravage your lips, sucking on the bottom one just a little until you moan, then I'll turn you around..."

"And?" She had to admit she was enjoying this little game they played.

"And I will unbutton your top button, and then the next one, placing a chaste kiss on your spine for each button I undo as I follow the path all the way down..." His hand, slid from her thigh around to her back, tracing a line from the middle of her back down to the chair before settling at the curves of her bottom and stroking her until she squirmed.

She suddenly had the urge to tear up the staircase, run into the room, and rip her clothes off.

"I'll set you on the edge of the bed and slowly remove your stockings, caressing each leg down to your toes. And when I finish, I'll pull you to your feet so I can untie the ribbons in the front of your shift. This will be the most difficult task I will have to complete."

She swallowed hard. "Why?"

"Because I'll finally get to do what I have oft dreamt of doing." His eyes danced as he met her gaze.

"You have? What have you dreamed about?"

He leaned into her ear, and with the lightest of a breath, whispered, "Caressing your breasts." Her shoulder reacted, pulling in toward her ear, and she gazed out at the group in front of her, but all seemed oblivious to what was unfolding on the dais.

She sat up straight and smiled, "And what do you do in all your dreams?"

"I carefully tug on the ribbons until your soft mounds are free of the material, and I allow your shift to fall to the ground. Then I do not know what to do next because I'm so excited." He took her hand and pulled it under the table so she could feel his hardness through his plaid. "See what you have done to me, wife?"

She grinned and pulled her hand back. "Go on. What do you do next?"

"First, I gaze at you, enjoying the sight of you with naught on in all your beauty—your long legs, the soft curve of your waist, the heavy weight of each breast, and your rosy lips. Then I will cup my hands under your breasts so I can feel the weight of them, the smoothness of your skin. Och, they will be perfect, so perfect that I will be unable to stop myself from rubbing my thumbs across your nipples until I bring them to hard peaks."

She leaned closer to his ear and whispered, "My nipples are already hard."

And he groaned.

Her father's head spun around, and suddenly he was staring directly at both of them. He made his way toward the dais, and whispered, "Come with me."

Tormod's alarmed look nearly broke her heart. "Do not worry. He's my sire and he likes you."

He muttered in her ear, "Naught could stop an erection faster than your father staring at me, I can promise you that."

Her father yelled to the crowd, "We'll be back in a short time. Carry on. I have something to give them." At the last minute, he tugged on Molly's mother's hand and said, "Come along, Gwynie." They moved slowly to accommodate her mother's limp, but she had improved in the short time since the battle.

Logan led the way through the courtyard and over to the stables, yelling to the lads as soon as he was close enough. "Lads, the horses. Where are they?"

The lads hurried to do what they were bade, bringing three horses to them. Her father turned to her and said, "Ride with your husband."

As they rode through the gates, Tormod whispered in her ear, "Where is he taking us? Should I be worried?"

"Do not be worried. I trust my mother and father, but I know not where we are headed." They shot out over the field, the wind chilling her to the bone, but she did not care. She was wrapped in Tormod's warm arms, and she loved him so much it surprised her every morn when she awakened.

Her father stopped in front of a small cottage she did not recall seeing.

Made of stone and a thatched roof, it was taller than many and was covered with pine and other greenery, something she'd never seen before.

Once Tormod helped her down, the door flew open and Maggie came running out, followed by Sorcha and Brigid. Gavin stood next to the door, his arms crossed and a satisfied smile on his face.

"We thought you'd never leave, Molly," cried Maggie, wrapping her arms around her sister's neck. "What took you so long?"

Her father barked, "Your sister was busy giving big doe eyes to her new husband. Never mind, get on with it."

Maggie grabbed one of her hands and tugged her inside. "We did this for you. This is your new home, yours and Tormod's. Mayhap you'll let me visit sometime."

"Me, too!" Brigid yelled.

Molly stepped inside, her hand still entwined with Tormod's. Together, they stepped into the most beautiful cottage she'd ever seen. Candles decorated the wall and the tables, freshly braided rushes dressed the floor, and the two chairs in front of the stone hearth were upholstered with thick cushions.

Off to the side was a table with shelving above it designed as a worktable. Another table and four stools sat in the center of the room, and Molly noticed a doorway in the corner.

Sorcha tugged on her hand. "Look, Molly, Papa even made you your own bedchamber. He bought you a big chest and a table and Mama had several of the softest rabbit pelts I've ever felt sewn together for you, like a blanket."

Molly looked at the bedchamber and burst into tears. "Papa, Mama, many thanks." She gave her father and mother each a hug, and Tormod thanked them, too.

Her mother pointed out a basket of food they'd brought, and Logan set a bottle of wine and two goblets on the table for them. "Special from Edinburgh." He then turned to his other daughters and yelled, "Time to go. Everyone out!"

Her sire was the last to leave. He turned around before he closed the door. "I wish you many happy years together. Molly, your brother and I will keep the troublemakers away. You'll not be bothered. Come visit in a few days."

CHAPTER TWENTY-FOUR

TORMOD SAID, "WE'VE BEEN BLESSED many ways. This is beautiful, Molly."

She nodded, still walking in a circle and fingering everything in the hut—dried flowers, a bowl of berries, candle holders, linens. "I cannot believe 'tis ours."

He poured her a goblet of wine and said, "Come, sit with me. Have one glass of wine and talk with me before…"

"Before?" She glanced up at him, and everything in him wanted to reach out and touch her pink cheeks.

"Before I take you into that room and do everything I promised to do."

She took a few sips of wine and whispered, "Let's skip ahead to you undressing me."

Tormod couldn't believe his ears, but he was not going to ask her to repeat herself. True, her sire had cooled his desires in an instant, but seeing Molly out of her dress was sure to bring them back in another instant.

He took her goblet in one hand, laced his hand with hers, and led her into the bedchamber. Once there, he set the goblet on the chest. "Here is your wine, lass. Turn around and I'll get started."

She pulled her hair to the front and gave him her back. "Will you tell me all you'll do?"

He unfastened the first button and kissed the nape of her neck. She shivered.

"Are you cold, lass?"

"Nay."

"I may not tell you all I'll do, because—" he kissed the next spot down her back, "—I may not think on it until I wish to do it. You do affect my mind that way." Once he finished the line of her back and dropped the gown to the floor, he moved forward until her back touched him. "I already forgot one thing."

She peeked over her shoulder at him, blushing to be only in her shift. "What?"

"I forgot to tell you that I wish to release your hair from its bindings. I wish to see it down around you so I can run my fingers through it." She helped him remove the flowers and the bindings, then tipped her head back, letting her long locks free. At first, he simply ran his fingers through her hair, but then he massaged her scalp until she moaned.

"Tormod, that feels wonderful."

When he finished, he reached around her and untied the first ribbon at the top of her shift, then paused to cup her breasts through the thin material. He groaned and turned her to face him, lowering his head to her nipple, taking the already taut bud in his mouth. He heard her intake of breath as she arched against him, pushing her breast further into his mouth.

He stood and said, "Enough with this." He quickly untied the ribbons and dropped the shift to the floor. He gazed at her as promised, taking her beauty in slowly, and whispered, "Have you any idea how lovely you are, my sweet wife?" He gazed into her innocent eyes, so trusting, so loving, and he was undone. His mouth descended on hers and he ravished it, suckling, teasing, parting her until they were both panting.

"Och, you'll make me lose it like a laddie."

Again, her doe eyes looked up at him.

He said, "Change of plans. With all the teasing we did before, I know not how long I can stand the torture." He lifted her into his arms, pulled the covers back, and placed her in the bed.

"What torture?"

He removed his plaid and his leine in quick order, then lowered himself on top of her, settling himself on his elbows and between her thighs. "The torture of not being inside you. The torture of watching you all these days and not being able to make you mine, to love you and worship you." He teased her bottom lip, nipping at her lightly. "You know 'twill hurt the first time. I'll do my best to not make it too much for you."

He waited to make sure she understood, then brought his hand up to cup her breast again, teasing her nipple with his thumb. "I must get you ready."

"How will you do that?"

He grinned as his hand slid down to the vee between her legs, teasing her before moving slowly inside her passage. "You are an inquisitive wee minx, are you not? I love everything about you, and I love that you're mine. If a lass is excited, her sheath gets wet—it will make it easier for me to slide into you, and it will make it more pleasant for you."

"You promise it will be pleasant for me?"

"I cannot promise the first time will be pleasant, but I promise the others will be."

Her hands ran down his arms, then over his hips before she reached down to wrap her palm around his erection.

He gasped when she touched him. "Do you like it when I touch you?" she whispered.

"Aye, verra much."

Her hand moved up and down, mimicking the movement he was making inside her with his fingers. "Do you like this?" she asked.

"Aye." He plunged his finger inside her again, pleased to see how slick she was already, so he entered another finger inside her. He was losing all sense of control. He leaned down to suckle her breast, and her legs opened wider, allowing him better access to her core. He could hear her panting, feel her need rising, and he wished to push her further.

She finally said, "If only the first time will hurt, then please do it now, so we can move on to the pleasurable part."

He groaned again, moved above her and grasped her hips, thrusting inside her with one push, breaking her barrier on impact. He could feel her tighten around him, then attempt to close her legs on him.

"Nay, stop."

"Hush, sweeting. I know it hurts, but I'll wait until you're ready."

She did as he said. "Promise it will get better?"

"Aye, but I will not move again until you tell me to." He gritted his teeth, struggling not to do what every part of his body begged him to do.

She moved tentatively against him twice, then one more time. "Tormod, 'tis better."

He thanked the Lord for that small favor and buried himself inside her before pulling out slowly and burying himself again. After a few times, he could feel her meeting his rhythm, her juices were flowing, and he heard some soft sounds from the back of her throat.

His own panting had reached a feverish pitch, but he vowed to wait for her since she was moving along with him. He whispered into her ear, "Let go, love. Go over the edge, I promise you'll love it, just let go."

And she did, groaning and clutching him, her insides contracting on him, pulling him along with her into an orgasm unlike any he'd ever felt.

He did his best not to collapse on her, instead staying up on his elbows and nuzzling her neck until he was able to speak.

"Tormod?"

"Aye?"

"Do that again."

CHAPTER TWENTY-FIVE

MOLLY AND TORMOD HAD TRAVELED a long way for this journey. She hadn't been sure about this trip, but Tormod and her father
had convinced her to do it. She'd invited her parents along, but they had
declined.

Her father had said he'd kill someone if he came with them, and her
mother had said she'd do something she wouldn't want her daughter and
new son-in-law to bear witness to, so Molly had accepted that as explanation enough. Maggie had also been invited but had staunchly refused.

Tormod helped her down from her horse. He kissed her forehead,
grabbed her hand, and whispered, "Are you ready?"

She nodded.

Tormod knocked on the door and a booming voice yelled, "Who is
it?"

Rather than wait for an invitation, Tormod stepped inside and said,
"Good eve to you. I bring your daughter Molly for a visit."

Molly's eye searched the chamber in the small English manor home.
The table needed cleaning and the floor was covered in filth, so much
so that she hated stepping in it. Once her eyes adjusted, she noticed her
father sitting in a chair at the end of the table. His hair was gone, and
he'd put on weight. There was a male seated on either side of him—she
guessed them to be her eldest brothers. Her mother was nowhere to be
seen.

The man grumbled, "I did have a daughter Molly, but I sold her.
There was not a man alive who would have her, so I sold her, along with

her sister. I care not for either of them. Their other sister was the only pretty one. Too bad she died when she was with child. This lass in front of me is certainly not Molly. Molly was ugly as a goat." The lads sitting with him snorted.

How Molly wished to react to him, but she did not. Now she understood him for what he was, a cruel, selfish man who was not worth her time.

To her surprise, Tormod flew down the table and lifted her father into the air. "You'll not speak disrespectfully about my wife."

"Tormod? Forget him. We can go now." Molly knew it had been a mistake to come here, but she'd wished to see her mother one last time, to make peace with her.

Tormod set her father back down and said, "Nay, we will not leave until I'm done."

"Done with what?" her father asked, his beady eyes still staring at her.

"With you. That is your daughter Molly, the most beautiful and giving woman I've ever met. She outshot every man with her bow and arrow and was the only one to capture and kill a blackguard who had eluded all of Scotland for many moons. She brought two men down with her arrows, saved two wee lassies, and became a favorite of King Alexander III. Shame on you for not treating her the way she deserved to be treated, but I can see it was best for her to get the hell away from you."

One brother said, "Papa, all we heard was true. Our sister is renowned."

"Be quiet." Her father pointed to her brother, pushed back and stood up from his chair. "Stay away from me. She deserved it, she was ug..."

Tormod lunged for him again. Grabbing the man by the neck, he landed his fist in his face. "Do not ever say that about her again." Neither of her brothers moved, both shocked by Tormod's behavior.

"Mama, where is Mama?" Molly asked, not the least bit concerned about her sire.

"She's in her bed. Lazy arse she is." Her sire pointed toward the next chamber.

Tormod whispered to her, "Go see your mama. I'll handle him."

Molly slipped into the next chamber while her father continued to rant about how wrong Tormod was because she could not be his daughter. Once her eyes adjusted to the darkness, she noticed a person in the bed, not moving. "Mama?"

Her mother's head lifted before it fell back onto the pillow. "Who's there?"

Molly moved over to the bed, lighting a candle next to it.

Her mother stared at her. Molly knew when recognition dawned on her. "Oh, saints preserve us. Molly? Have I finally passed on? Is it truly you?"

"Aye, Mama. 'Tis me. Your eldest daughter. Nay, you have not passed, you are here with me." She moved into the light so her mother could see her better.

"Oh, heavens above. 'Tis nearly my time, lass. I am sure of it." Her hand moved toward Molly's cheek. "Look at you, you are more lovely than any girl I've ever seen."

"My thanks, Mama. What is wrong? Why are you still abed?"

Her mother's breathing sounded raspy and laborious. She grabbed Molly's hand. "Thank you...for...coming to see me. I'm so sorry...felt awful all these years. So guilty. I should have..." She broke into a fit of coughing, a nasty cough that would probably take her soon.

Her head fell back on the pillow and she stared up at the ceiling, still fighting to breathe. "I'd so hoped to see you again. How is...Maggie?"

"Maggie is wonderful. She could not come."

"You sound...like...the Scots."

"Mama, I am a Scot now. I was adopted by a wonderful family."

Her mother's hand, little more than skin on bone, reached up to her cup her cheek. "Forgive me. I've been sick for so long, but I'd hoped... to...see you...before...I always loved you both..."

Her mother stared off to the side.

Molly covered her mother's hand with hers. "Mama?"

"Forgive me...'tis time, I've waited so long for you...my thanks for coming to see an old woman..." She stared over Molly's shoulder, taking a few more shallow breaths until her eyes closed.

And she knew someday soon her mother would take her last breath. She kissed her brow and covered her with the blanket. "I love you, Mama. I know you did not wish to send us away. I forgive you, and we've lived a wonderful life."

Her mother's eyes fluttered open. "My thanks. My time is near, and now I can go with my heart at peace. I worried so..."

Molly sat on a stool nearby watching her mother as she slept, fighting for each breath she took in. She held her mother's hand while she hummed a song she recalled from her childhood. Her mother had such a lovely voice. How odd that she remembered it so well, yet Maggie had few memories of their time at home. After a while, she said a few prayers and moved back out to the front room, her own soul at rest now for coming to see her mother.

One of her brothers moved forward to look at her more closely, though he made no move to greet her. "Papa, I think it is Molly."

He bolted out of his chair and barked, "It is not Molly. Take yourselves out of here."

"Tormod, we can take our leave. I have made peace with my mother, and I'm glad I came." She kissed Tormod's cheek. "Do not waste any more time on my sire. He is not worth any effort. Many thanks, husband." She swiped a tear from her cheek before she headed out the door.

They moved back out to their horses, and Tormod lifted her onto hers. "Are you ready, my love?"

She leaned down to give him a quick kiss. "Aye, I am."

Tormod climbed on his horse and flicked the reins.

"Take me home, husband."

A sennight later, Tormod and Molly had been called to the keep by Molly's sire. They chattered with a few people in the great hall before stepping into her uncle's solar. "What is it, Papa?"

A large man Tormod didn't recognize was standing and studying the weapons mounted on the wall—the weapons of his wife's ancestors. Gwyneth Ramsay sat in one of the chairs, a wide smile on her face.

Molly frowned as soon as she saw her mother, but Tormod wasn't sure why. Was she suspicious? Did she know this man who had his back to them?

Tormod rubbed his hand on the back of his neck, suddenly worried.

The stranger spun on his heel and said, "Greetings, both of you, and congratulations on your success in taking down the most elusive villain the Scots have seen in many years. Why do you not sit down?" He held his hand out, indicating where he wished them to sit, so Molly took one of the chairs and Tormod sat opposite her.

Molly's sire stood in his usual position, leaning against Quade's desk, his arms crossed in front of him. "Molly, Tormod, I'd like you to meet Mr. Hamilton. This is the gentleman your mother and I have dealt with in our work for the Scottish Crown."

Molly glanced at Tormod—a silent question—and he shrugged his shoulders. But then something occurred to him. This was the man who was in charge of the spies and their activities. Could he be, was it possible...? Tormod could not stop the grin from erupting on his face at the thought of what this man might be about to ask them. He glanced at Molly again, but it was clear she still did not know what to make of the unexpected visit.

He gave his attention back to Mr. Hamilton, who was still talking. "'Struth is, your performance impressed me so much, I knew I had to meet you."

Molly nodded, a blank expression still on her face.

He sat at the table and folded his hands in front of him. "You remind me of two verra special people, and I'm here to ask you if you would be willing to work alongside them."

"Special people? I do not understand." Molly said, glancing from her sire to her mother and then back at Tormod.

"Spies. My best people are your sire and your mother, who, I must admit, are quite magical together. So much so they've inspired me to make an offer to the two of you."

Molly's mouth dropped open.

"Tormod, would you and your lovely wife, Molly, be willing to work for the Scottish Crown in the same capacity her parents have been doing for me for many years? They would be part of your training as well. I want you to be trained by the verra best."

Tormod immediately turned to his wife and asked, "What do you think, Molly?"

"You're asking us to work for the Crown, the same as my parents?" Molly's tone made it clear she was as shocked as he was.

Her sire, about to explode, came over and squeezed both of them.

"Come be spies with your mama and me, Molly. You'll love it."

All Molly could do was nod.

Tormod kissed her cheek and whispered, "All your dreams have come true, love." And suddenly, he realized something else. So had his.

He loved being part of the Ramsay clan almost as much as he loved his wife. They were warm and loving people, much like the Grants. He understood why they were such strong allies. Their philosophies were similar, and they were kind to everyone in their clan.

He hadn't missed his sire and brother one bit, nor had he longed for their approval. Nay, he wished to stay here by Molly's side forever.

She whispered in his ear, "Nay, all of *our* dreams have come true."

How fortunate they were. He nodded to Mr. Hamilton. "We'd be honored to work for the Scottish Crown."

He wrapped his arm around his wife and she said, "I am so happy, husband."

As was he.

Together, they were so, so blessedly happy.

EPILOGUE

JAMIE GRANT WAS RESTLESS.

Aye, he'd been happy for many, many years. He loved his family so. He had been fortunate to be one of the twins born to Laird Alexander Grant and his wife, Maddie. He adored all his siblings: his twin brother Jake, born just before him; his sisters, Kyla, Eliza, and Maeve; and his youngest brother, Connor. He had more cousins than he could count, and his favorite time of year was the annual Ramsay festival.

But things had changed.

Jake was married now, and happier than Jamie had ever seen him. Jake's friend Magnus had married his cousin Ashlyn, who'd sworn never to marry. Ashlyn's joy had transformed her into a completely different person. She no longer pushed people away.

Then he'd traveled to Edinburgh with Tormod, Coll, and Braden, and word had just reached them that Tormod and Molly were now married.

And how could he forget that his cousins, Torrian and Lily, were both married, too?

He stood on the parapets next to his father, glancing over his sire's land, land that would someday belong to his brother Jake.

"'Tis your land, too, Jamie," his father whispered, as if reading his thoughts.

He swung his head to stare at his father. "I did not say aught."

"I know, but my guess is you were thinking on it, were you not?"

Jamie decided to change the topic of conversation. "I was thinking on all the changes that have taken place as of late."

"Aye, your brother has taken a wife." His father stared straight ahead. "He's verra happy."

Jamie nodded, turning his attention back to the landscape.

"As is Magnus. Torrian, also." He clasped Jamie's shoulder with an affectionate squeeze.

"And Lily," Jamie added. "In fact, Lily just gave birth to her twin lassies. I heard Kyle fell off the stool."

"Aye, 'tis true. She named them Lise and Liliana." His father smiled as he gazed out over his land, but then he turned to Jamie again. "Do not forget your cousin Loki."

"Saints above. I forgot about Loki. Am I the only one who has not taken a wife?"

His father chuckled, "Nay, neither Connor nor Braden nor Roddy have been so inclined. There are plenty of Ramsays who have yet to wed, and none of your sisters have mentioned an interest, though Kyla is of age. But you know what your mother says..."

Jamie pivoted to face his father again. "Nay. What does Mama say?"

His sire smirked and waggled his eyebrows at his son.

"She says you're next."

THE END

NOVELS BY
KEIRA MONTCLAIR

The Clan Grant Series
#1- RESCUED BY A HIGHLANDER-Alex and Maddie
#2- HEALING A HIGHLANDER'S HEART-Brenna and Quade
#3- LOVE LETTERS FROM LARGS-Brodie and Celestina
#4-JOURNEY TO THE HIGHLANDS-Robbie and Caralyn
#5-HIGHLAND SPARKS-Logan and Gwyneth
#6-MY DESPERATE HIGHLANDER-Micheil and Diana
#7-THE BRIGHTEST STAR IN THE HIGHLANDS-Jennie and Aedan
#8- HIGHLAND HARMONY-Avelina and Drew

The Highland Clan
LOKI-Book One
TORRIAN-Book Two
LILY-Book Three
JAKE-Book Four
ASHLYN-Book Five
MOLLY-Book Six

The Summerhill Series- Contemporary Romance
#1-ONE SUMMERHILL DAY
#2-A FRESH START FOR TWO

Regency
THE DUKE AND THE DRESSMAKER

D EAR READERS,

Thanks for reading!

I hope you enjoyed my sixth novel in THE HIGHLAND CLAN series, *Molly*. If you are interested in learning more about Molly's younger days, she was discovered by Gwyneth Ramsay tethered to a tree in *My Desperate Highlander*, Micheil and Diana's story. Aunt Avelina's story is told in *Highland Harmony*.

At the end of this, I have included a short excerpt from *My Desperate Highlander* when we first met Molly.

In my books, I love to point out some of the modern conveniences we take for granted in our lives. One of the conveniences they lacked in England and Scotland in the 1200s was the mirror. Can you imagine, ladies, never being able to check your reflection?

Molly spent her entire life avoiding her reflection, whether in a serene lake or a piece of metal or a shiny rock because her biological father had convinced her she was homely. The rock in the cave was black obsidian, found in Scotland, which can actually show your reflection because it looks like dark glass. France and Italy were first credited with creating glass and then the mirror, according to my research, but the only way to obtain something from across the water was usually through a traveling priest. Two years is probably a realistic amount of time, though since I did not live in those times, I cannot say for sure.

As always, I write fiction, and I create based on the best research I can find, which doesn't necessarily make it fact. There is still much we don't know about medieval Scotland (or the land of the Scots since it was still part of England).

If you want to know more about my novels, here are some places for you to visit.

Visit my website at www.keiramontclair.com and sign up for my newsletter. I'll keep you updated about my new releases without bothering you often.

Go to my Facebook page and 'like' me: You will get updates on any new novels, book signings, and giveaways. https://www.facebook.com/KeiraMontclair

Stop by my Pinterest page:
http://www.pinterest.com/KeiraMontclair/ You'll see how I envision Molly and Tormod.

Leave a review on Amazon or Goodreads. Reviews help self-published authors like me and help other readers as well.

Happy reading!

Keira Montclair

www.keiramontclair.com

ABOUT THE AUTHOR

KEIRA MONTCLAIR IS THE PEN name of an author who lives in Florida with her husband. She loves to write fast-paced, emotional romance, especially with children as secondary characters in her stories.

She has worked as a registered nurse in pediatrics and recovery room nursing. Teaching is another of her loves, and she has taught both high school mathematics and practical nursing.

Now she loves to spend her time writing, but there isn't enough time to write everything she wants! Her Highlander Clan Grant series, comprising of eight standalone novels, is a reader favorite. Her third series, The Highland Clan, set twenty years after the Clan Grant series, focuses on the Grant/Ramsay descendants. She also has a contemporary series set in The Finger Lakes of Western New York.

You may contact her through her website at **www.keiramontclair. com.** She also has a Facebook account and a twitter account through Keira Montclair. If you send her an email through her website, she promises to respond.

Read on for a short excerpt from the middle of
My Desperate Highlander:

Chapter Fourteen

WHEN MICHEIL ARRIVED BACK AT the home, Logan and Gwyneth were already there with a young dark-haired lass around ten or eleven summers. He stopped as soon as he stepped inside the door, frozen in place by the sight of the bruises on the young girl's face.

Micheil stared at Logan with his eyebrows raised in question. Gwyneth sat in the corner feeding Sorcha.

Logan placed his hands on the lassie's shoulders. "This is Molly. Molly worked for the English family that brought Randall Baines and his betrothed here to town."

"But no longer?" Micheil asked.

"Nay. Molly dropped a trencher on the floor, and the grandmother of Clarice, the girl to be married, slapped her and ordered for her to be beaten with a switch. Gwynie found her outside sobbing after her beating. Ena, the grandmother, thought if they sent her out into the cold without any protection, she would learn her lesson better. She was tethered to a tree."

Molly hung her head, tears rolling down her cheeks in humiliation.

Aunt Elspeth said, "Molly, please do not cry. I promise we will never beat you."

Micheil said, "Nay, we will not beat you. Where are your parents?"

"In England," Logan answered. "Tell Micheil why they sent you away," he added, his voice gentle.

Her gaze remained staring at the floor. "My sire said there were too many mouths to feed, so my younger sister and I were sent out. He wouldn't part with his sons."

"Where is your sister?" Micheil was almost afraid to ask.

"Maggie is still inside." Her eyes turned hopeful at the mention of her sister.

"Do you have information about Diana, a lady with red hair?"

Logan smiled. "Why, aye, she does. Molly can lead us to Diana. She knows exactly where she is being kept. Diana was kidnapped to be taken back to England as Randall Baines's mistress." He tipped his head at his brother.

Micheil's eyes widened. Lord, he could hardly believe it, but judging from the expression on Logan's face, it was true. "His mistress?"

Molly nodded, her eyes still cast down. "His new wife agreed."

Micheil knelt in front of the lass and placed his finger under her chin, forcing her to look into his eyes. "My thanks, Molly, for helping us. Is Lady Diana alive and well?"

"Aye, they have her guarded until Randall returns from the wedding ceremony."

Gwyneth announced, "We also have another job to do."

"And that is?" Micheil asked.

"We're going to find Maggie and bring her with us. I have need of a couple of helpers with my bairn, especially since my husband has made me with child again." She glared at Logan. "Molly said she would prefer to go with us instead of back to England with that family. Logan and I thought it was a wonderful idea."

Molly spoke up. "I can clean clothes, too, my lord." She stood stiff as a board, not moving a muscle, probably sore from her beating.

Micheil stared into space, envisioning wrapping his hands around Baines's neck so he could choke him slowly. "That sounds wonderful, Gwyneth. I think Molly and Maggie will like the Ramsay keep, and I'm sure Mama would love to have them."

"Come eat more, lassie," Aunt Elspeth said, grabbing Molly by the hand. "You are too thin." She sat her down at the table, but Molly jumped back out of the chair.

"Must I sit, my lady?" Her hands protected her backside.

Elspeth found a soft plaid and set it atop the chair. "Try this, lass."

Micheil spun around to Gwyneth. "Are you two ready? 'Tis time to prepare ourselves and do this." He wrung his hands as he stood in the middle of the small hall.

He just couldn't wait any longer. How the hell could someone take a switch to such a wee lass? "And Molly? Do not forget to show us which one is the grandmother who ordered your punishment."

My Desperate Highlander,
the sixth in the Clan Grant series.

Made in the USA
Lexington, KY
12 August 2017